FROM VIRGIN STREAM

FROM VIRGIN STREAM

ROBERT FALLON

Matador
5 Weir Road
Kibworth
Leicester LE8 0LQ
0116 2792299
Email: books@troubador.co.uk
Web: www.troubador.co.uk/matador

ISBN: 9781848762510

Typeset in 12pt Stempel Garamond by Troubador Publishing Ltd, Leicester, UK

Matador is an imprint of Troubador Publishing Ltd

CONTENTS

On The Subject Of Death and Life After

FOREWORD

The author would like to thank the Editor of the *Leicester Mercury* newspaper in August 2008 who gave him permission to publish the opening short story in verse. The thought provoking story was found in a bedside locker at Leicester Royal Infirmary after the death of an old lady in the bed alongside. It was sent to the newspaper by a reader and published in the newspaper's Mr Leicester's Diary.

INTRODUCTION

A compilation of stories in verse which take in the reader on a roller coaster ride through human emotion, behaviour, achievement and failings, from Adam and Eve to death and beyond.

Author Robert Fallon was born in the coal mining village of Lochore in the county of Fife in Scotland. He has lived for most of his adult life in Leicester, in England. Author of the early leaning book for children titled *The Itsy Bitsy Family* and the novel for older children *The Dream Maker*. He is also a published short story writer and award winning contemporary poet in the hardbacked book of poems entitled *Modern Times*.

LEICESTER MERCURY DIARY

What do you think you see,
nurses, what do you think
you see?
Are you thinking when you
are looking at me?
A crabbit old woman, not
very wise,
Uncertain of habit, with far
away eyes,
Who dribbles her food and
makes no reply,
When you say in a loud voice
'do wish you'd try'
Who seems not to notice the
things that you do
And forever is losing a
stocking or shoe,
Who resisting or not lets
you do as you will
With bathing and feeding
the long day to fill.
Is that what you're thinking?
Is that what you see?
Then open your eyes nurse,
you're not looking at me.
I'd tell you who I am as I
sit here so still,
As I move at your bidding, as
I eat at your will.

1

I'm a small child of ten with
a father and mother,
Brothers and sisters who love
one another.
A young girl of sixteen with
wings on her feet
Dreaming that soon now a
lover she'll meet.
A bride soon at twenty my
heart gives a leap
Remembering the vows that
I promised to keep,
At twenty-five now I have
young of my own
Who need me to build a
secure happy home.
A woman of thirty, my young
now grow fast
Bound to each other with ties
that should last.
At forty, my young sons
now grown, will be gone
But my man stays beside me
to see I don't mourn,
At fifty once more babies
play around my knee,
Again we know children my
loved one and me.
Dark days are upon me, my
husband is dead.
I look to the future, I
shudder with dread.
My young are all busy rearing
young of their own
And I think of the years and
the love that I've known
I'm an old woman now and
nature is cruel,

Tis her jest to make old age
look like a fool.
The body it crumbles, grace
and vigour depart
There is now a stone where
once was a heart.
But inside this old body a
young girl still dwells
And now and again my
battered heart swells.
I remember the joys, I
remember the pain,
And I'm loving and living all
over again.
I think of the years all
too few – gone so fast
And accept the fact that
nothing will last.
So open your eyes, nurse,
open and see
Not a crabbit old woman
look closer – see me.

HUMAN NATURE

POETIC JUSTICE

All of life's emotions
Created in the head
Saved for prosperity
By writing to digest.
Clearing of the conscience
With no physical intent
Waves away depression
To your journey's end.
From enlightenment to poison
The pen reveals the mind
To those who read and judge
Words sometimes set to rhyme.

TYPIST

A lady I did not know
My words through friend
In type once set.
Number of lines
She put right top
Top left pen name
Address full stop.
With deft hands
Single or double spacing.
When of politicians, police
I had my say
Did she think
'you're right you know'
Was she blushing
And in shock
When my mind
With sex would toy?
I don't want answers
To these things
In case her words
my ego stings.

HUMANS

With bounty gifted
Brain and health
But basic instinct
To kill self.
From bullet, torture
And the bomb
Exudes a melancholy form.
No plague of locusts
In pursuit
Destructs the earth
As does man's boots.

DIGNITY

In certain state of mind
For some the price is high,
Forever nose aimed at the sky
With downward stoop of eye.
In small amounts
It gives the scope
Pleasure in life to adopt,
But few get the balance right
To keep in check malicious spite.

ENVY

The grass is greener
On the other side
Is envy view
From troubled mind
But all that glitters
Is not gold
From barren land
Black riches flow.

NOSEY PARKERS

Your private life
Not left alone
Until some gossip
They have sown.
It does not matter
How you live
Alone or in a crowd
Married, single or divorced
They will pry and probe
Until they find some matter
To give your life a jolt.

MISBEHAVIOUR

What this seems
To self-righteous one
To broader mind is fun.
It stems from make-up
In your genes
By varied life
Find more esteem
For gender fulfilment
To enlight.

CONSCIENCE

Like a baby frog
In dormant state
Silently sits and waits
Its home is deep
Within the brain
To feed on guilt
Some drive insane.
As life span grows
So does this thing
Until large toad
Is living within
It wrinkles forehead
Bloats the skin
Will give no peace
Until heart gives in.

COMPUTER ERROR

He was a man aged forty two
Who went to Doctor feeling ill
In the waiting room he sat
With coughs and sneezes
All around.
Doctor's brain was in a mist
From smoking and booze,
Drugs and preservatives,
Also his elderly, death list.
He got a letter in the mail
Telling him he's now female
Go to maternity with full bladder
Do not strain your body either.
He did not know a change was on
The shock was all
A bit too strong
His name it seems is Gladys Jones
The beer belly now has cause to moan.

THE ULTIMATE COMPUTER

In inner box
lies a mind
To eat, digest
That fed inside,
Subconscious mixes
Up this brew
In bits and pieces
Sends dreams to you.
The centre box
A lump of grey
Commands with signals
All obey.
Outer box all tarted up
With a mouth to erupt
Above which
Two eyes to see
Between a nose
With which to sneeze.
Ears of two
Stick out of sides
To transfer noises
Into mind.
Scientific wonder
Is all this
Till virus inserted
When one sees fit.
The furore caused
In computer brain
Escapes the logic
Such mayhem.

TELEVISION

It's fixed on wall
Or stands in room
For imagination, oblivion.
On screen eyes are glued
To whatever channel
That you choose.
Adverts can break the spell
To eat something
Or get a drink.
It wills you then
To stare away.
You blink the lids
And yawn a lot.
Of those around unaware
A zombie on settee or chair
Soap operas, quiz shows
No matter what
Your brain on hold
Is now stuck
Till yourself
Become switched off.

TREADMILL

The treads are stiff
But hopes start high
Of get rich quick
Then at ease lie.
The harder tread
More material milk
Quicken the pace
For wealth in-built.
We can't get off
Just freely go
No brake on treadmill
Will not slow.
From tunnel vision
Creeps a tear
What have we lost
As treads do steer.

PROS AND CONS

For centuries have
Plied their trade
The world over
Pro ladies
Of the night
From street corners
To penthouse.
Persecuted, scorned
Through the years
By man and law alike
But they save many
From fall from grace
As they con punters
From ladies who
Straight laced appear.

SOLITUDE

To some it brings
Great apprehension
When walking into
Empty room or house
Or being in a public place
But not part of the crowd.
Can also give contentment
Space to think and observe
All manner of bounty
Here on planet earth.
From forest glade
In winter
Trees standing
Stark and bare
To buds of spring
The summer greens
And multi coloured
Autumn carpet
When the winds race
Through the trees.
A rainbow gives
Intimate contact
With a clearing sky.
On deserted beach
In moonlight rays
Waves washing rocks
And shoreline
Brings solitary peace
With deeper meaning
To your thoughts
And deeds.

THE CHISSETS

A tight knit community
English born and bred
Wary of strangers
In their midst
Now become a minority
On nearly every street
Swallowed up by strangers
Who speak in foreign tongues.
Some went to live
In Scotland
To take advantage of
Free medical prescriptions
And elderly care homes,
Others fled permanently
To their holiday east coast.
They are part of folklore there
In Skegness and Bridlington
Unlike the Scottish
Their thrift is no myth,
Knicknamed the Chissets
By traders along the coast
For even with price tag
On prominent display
'How much is it?' They ask, as fingers fiddle
Deep in purse,
With look of disbelief
And pout
As trader tells them
No discount.

MOP TOP BEAUTY

With hole at rear
Wears baseball hat
From which long pigtail
Falls down back,
Face of owner
Framed in this
Looks about
To have death kiss.
Eyes bloodshot
With water in,
Nose a dripping
On his chin.
Yellow stain
Covers teeth
Gaps from which
bad breath release.
One ear like
A cauliflower
From batterings
Has turned sour.
Skin is wrinkled
From years of want,
Even stubble
Looking gaunt,
Body stands
On twiggy limbs
Knee caps jutting
Out from shins.
The mystery

Of this story
How has hair
Kept all its glory.
Moral now
Must be said
Don't let beauty
Go to head.

MOODS

They come on waves
Of emotional tides
Many are good
But some so bad
Into deep depression
For days can sink.
When mood is dark
Be realistic
In your thoughts.
Think of the millions
In dire straits
From hunger and plights
Of the human race.
It is sad to say
But it cheers you up
That many have moods
Much darker than you
Or any human
Should endure.

HISTORICAL MIX

OPEN LETTER TO
President Obama
The White House
Washington D.C.
From the U.K.
March 2009.

Dear Sir,

You had our deep sympathy when you walked into the White House, to face the most appalling legacy left to any American President in recorded history. Events were reaching boiling point when President Bush escaped out of the White House back door. On the oval desk no doubt was evidence of his indiscretions, mistakes and maybe more. Two on going conflicts he left you, terrorist cells world wide. To top it all a recession from a Global meltdown, that started on your doorstep and might make furrows in your brow.

Are bankers in the U.S.A. and United Kingdom living in a fairy wonderland? They bankrupted their businesses with risky deals using clients cash, to award themselves bonuses of unbelievable size. Then had the nerve to dig into government hand-outs of taxpayers' hard-earned tax. In Britain we wonder if our politicians are treading the same path. With generations of sleaze stuck to their shoes and devious bending of Parliament's rules, making a hidden income from family employed staff and second homes not used. Brazen faced they then declare that they have done no wrong. We've got elected Peers filling their well-fed faces with question scams in the House of Lords. Now in this recession with millions out of work some of our politicians have the audacity to ask for a massive pay rise, now rule bending found out. No doubt this is to cover money they might lose from fiddling from the national purse if there is tightening of the rules.

The general opinion of the public here is politicians with guilt complexes are afraid to take the money men to court, in case for their own devious ways, they might yet have a price to pay. If the honest men and women at the heart of power, don't soon take a stand, against widespread corruption in their midst, national rebellions are more of a certainty than just a passing chance.

Some humble advice, Sir, that may ease the stress of your position. Don't try to force American idealism down the throats of other nations. Many of your predecessors did with tragic consequence. Vietnam is a prime example that President Bush should have heeded. After many years of anguish, death and destruction, communism won the day with America's embarrassing withdrawal. Now without any idealistic help Vietnam more democratic. The time has gone when any country can police or rule the world. Try to save the planet from its fate as human beings its resources rape...

HASTING's CUT OFF

California was their goal
From every country they did roll.
Hundreds of miles by wagon train
To end up eaten or insane.
Hasting's short cut was not planned
A route untrodden by this man.
If they had taken longer route
Would not have frozen in their boots
With safety just one ridge to climb
From mountain blizzard they took cover.
Wagons sunk in sea of salt
In Utah had held them up.
Oxen killed by Indian arrows
Those left gorged to bone and marrow.
Some did eat their next of kin
Flesh, heart and liver kept life within.
To the Garden of Eden a few survived
What price to pay to stay alive.
If you're named Donar or a Reid
Remember suffering of former creed.

THE BIG THREE

After the chaos of World War Two
At Yalta in the Ukraine a meeting took place
For the big three to carve up Europe
Questions are still on our lips
About all the suffering that came from this.
Stalin promised in Eastern States, Democracy he would decree.
Why did America and Britain trust the Russian Dictator
When knowing of his ruthless nature?
Should Roosevelt have been there, ill in his wheelchair
With just three months to live?
Was Churchill weary in his mind from fighting Hitler and Japan?
From signed agreement Europe was split
For decades millions suffered from it.
From behind barbed wire and concrete walls
Slaves to tyranny arose enmasse
When the Berlin Wall was breached
The Big Three at last were in retreat.

AMERICAN PRESIDENTS

They would like to be remembered
For their work as head of state
But some go down in history
For words or fibs from oval office.
President Truman's angry outburst
'If you can't stand the heat get out of the kitchen,'
When all around him got cold feet.
President Nixon's infamy, from one word
WATERGATE
Forced him to resign
He could have left the White House
As a great statesman
Dialogue with China he had just begun.
President Bush went to War
Assuming that Saddam
Had weapons of mass destruction
With his British shadow
Talked Nations into conflict.
President Clinton in office
Served with distinction
Until he announced with a straight face
'I did not have sex, with that woman'
Not impeached but in disgrace.

NINE-ELEVEN
SEPTEMBER HORROR

They stood in twin splendour
Monuments to human ingenuity
Shimmering in the morning haze
Above the urban sprawl.
Suicidal Jihad fanatics
Flew into the Towers that day
The world watched in disbelief
As second Tower was struck
Then both crumbled into dust,
Millions would count the cost.
No written words of any creed
Should by acts like this be blasphemed
Or those seeking religious direction
Be cloned by adult seed.
The aftermath brings misery
As eye to eye confronts
Terror with eternal goal
To jaws of hell is linked.

WILLIAM SHAKESPEARE

Will our master
Of the word
With each phrase
The mind to stir.
Through War and Peace
Your works live on
To feed each intellect
Weak or strong.
Shylock on to Macbeth,
Greed, lighthearted
To great depth.
Romeo with Juliet
Bleeds the hearts
As tears still wept.
Stratford-on-Avon
Your monument
With house a shrine
To ink and pen.
Students all,
Who search to write,
Will Shakespeare read
Pen to enlight.

WARWICK CASTLE

From earth rampart by Ethelfreda
In year 914
To present day as Castle stands
Its excellence supreme.
Invaded often through the years
By home and foreign foe
William the Conqueror
Is one that we all know.
Simon Demontfort of French noble birth
Who became Earl of Leicester
And brother in law to King.
The Beauchamp Dynasty began
In year 1268
It was the most significant
To Castle's present state
Richard Beauchamp, Captain of Calais
Built in strength to save.
Now Tussauds gives authenticity
To the many Castle rooms
With life size figures in period costume.
Wander in Peacock garden
Dungeons or Constable's room
See heart of England's history
In picture, dress and tomb.

SIMON DE MONTFORT

In 1229 this Frenchman came
Peacefully a part of Leicester claimed
As Earl of Leicester he did serve
Wed sister of King Henry the Third
Foremost soldier in Christendom
Governor of Gascony did become.
A man of determined zeal
Accused of having oppressive heel.
Resigned as Governor, returned to France.
When Gascons revolted rejoined Henry
Lost command to the King's son
Who later became King Edward the First.
Led group of Barons 1258
On Henry to enforce debate
At Battle of Lewes as history shows
Gave the Monarch a bloody nose.
Later killed in this Civil War
As Henry with his sword did score.
Clock tower statue, street name hung
Of Leicester's famous, French noble's son

BRADGATE PARK

By village of thatch and Swithland slate
A page of history lies in wait,
Past quaint church, across stone bridge
In Charnwood Forest's splendour sits.

Through its valley runs a stream
With waterfalls a tranquil scene,
Acre on acre the deer roam free
To feed on pasture next picnic tea.
Outcrops of granite the eyes to raise
From green to gold ferns by grass pathways.
Old oaks, stark, gnarled and thick,
With trees in dense foliage mix.
When covered in its winter coat
Gives virgin feel, so remote.

Once stately home now crumbling brick
Where 'Lady Jane Grey' once was chic,
Queen of England for days of nine
Then innocent head to axe reclined.

Its topmost hill is called 'Old John'
To honour man of peasant born,
With memorial stone tankard against the sky
His spirit walks with you and I.
The unspoilt scenery beneath John's gaze
In National Trust for Leicester stays.
A visit to this timeless zone
Refreshes mind as idly roam.

BATTLE OF BOSWORTH FIELD

August 1485 Richard III on Bosworth died
Plantagenets of York on banner borne
By Shakespeare in history scorned.
On horseback led his armoured knights
Last English king from fore to fight.
With coat of arms on shield did charge
Into the midst of warring mass
Later on that savage day
He crashed to ground from dead mount dazed.
'My kingdom for a horse' did shout
As overwhelmed by Richmond's might,
The House of Lancaster victory won
Henry VII reign begun.
Wars of the Roses now at end
Into Tudor Dynasty England blends.
With Hastings of 1066
And Battle of Britain with the blitz,
Bosworth Field in importance fits
In splendour of Leicestershire countryside
A feast awaits enquiring minds.

RICHARD THE THIRD

The gold to pay his troops
He left at Blue Boar Inn
Before he crossed Leicester's West Bridge
For Battle of Bosworth Field,
An old Hag screeched as he rode by
Your head will strike the bridge
When he passed safely over
He must have thought she's mad.
Later on that fateful day
He died on Battlefield
His body draped across a horse
To Leicester would be borne.
On the West Bridge, Hag's prophesy came true
His head a dangling struck the bridge
Throwing his body all askew.
Would he have left his gold behind?
If he had known that since his death
It never has been found.

WILLIAM WYGGESTON

Born in reign of Edward IV
To leave his mark on Leicester's course.
Son of a merchant of the wool
With staples at Calais on exports ruled.
Married twice with no heir
His bounty left for public care.
Founder of hospital in his name
And schools of high standards to acclaim
Chantry and almshouses also sprang
From hand of this religious man.
Lord Mayor more than once was he
Civil service ran through family tree.
Unlike his legacy, death date obscure
About 1513 left wealth to poor.
On clock tower his statue stands
To look on us for whom he planned.

CARDINAL WOLSEY
BORN 1471

From butcher's son to Cardinal grew
With palaces to fit his grace
At Hampton Court and York House stayed.
Greatest reformer of his time
In Civil Law a cause did find.
For treason summoned by Henry VIII
From York to London made his way
At Leicester Abbey for overnight stop
Did prophecy there his bones would rot.
Three days later died as he said
Peacefully in his Abbey bed.
Henry in act of revenge
Burned Leicester Abbey to the ground.
Cardinal Wolsey, Archbishop of York
Where now lies your coffin plot
Of your grave there is no trace
Did Henry order to desecrate?

THE CIVIL WAR

Eleven years of bloodshed Religion to redress
The Church of Rome outlawed, this led to civil war,
For future generations Democracy at stake.
Puritans known as Roundheads, backed Cromwell's Parliament
Anglicans as Cavaliers, for Charles the First the King.
In Battle of Edgehill in 1642
Nearly thirty thousand combatants fought: from dawn to dusk.
The thrust and shouts of Pikemen, shots of Musketeers
A charge with swords by Cavalry, but no victor would be clear.
The Battles would be many, Gloucester, Naseby, Marston Moor
To name just a few.
In Worcester Campaign of 1651, a decisive victory Cromwell won
But victory was hollow for at a later date
To keep the peace compromised, the Crown and Mace both stayed.
Freedom of Religion now deemed the right of all
This was not meant to be the outcome, did Battles end in draw?
Through Sealed Knot Society, debate still rages on
Mock Battles giving vent to passions still held strong.

ALDERMAN GABRIEL NEWTON

Born around 1684
A Leicester benefactor of renown.
At Horse and Trumpet inn was host
To weary travellers from horse and coach.
From meeting of so many souls
Education for poor idea took hold
Founder of Alderman Newton School
To teach the poor for life more full.
Keen interest had he in civic affairs
Served Leicester as Mayor, a man who cared.
With religion he was possessed
Each day at church atoned with zest.
Educational, charitable foundations made
To benefit the human race.
In 1762 he drew last breath
At All Saints church was laid to rest.
Humanitarian with strong religious views
With deep respect sir, we honour you.

DANIEL LAMBERT

Born 1770 this Leicester son
To become in girth the largest one
His belongings from furniture to portraits
In Newarke House Museum stay.
Of normal stature till twenty two
An average diet he ate, it's true
Active in sports was known to be
Bred dogs and fighting cocks for fee.
Then the weight began to roll
On to him with increasing fold.
A shilling sufficed to see this man
As on exhibition he toured the land
Fifty stone upward he did weigh
Nine feet of fat around waist lay
Died suddenly in 1809.
A score of men sweated and groaned
To lower his body to earthly home
In St. Martins churchyard at Stamford lies
Large grave looked on with curious eyes.

ROBIN HOOD

As sung in ancient ballads
Robin Hood is hard to place
To Barnsdale in Yorkshire
His movements have been traced.
In historic documents
Robin Hood's name can be seen
On court of rolls at Wakefield
Plus Northamptonshire was penned.
Sherwood Forest it appears
Was his main abode
A deadly shot with longbow
Added to folklore.
An elusive figure dressed in green
Was outlaw Robin Hood
He killed the royal deer
Stole from travellers rich
To help impoverished peasants
Taxed beyond belief.
The sheriff of Nottingham
Was his arch enemy
Brought about by unjust laws
To please the sport of kings.
Royal forest wardens
Would kill or mutilate
Any who killed forest deer
Or possessed a part of take.
A legend in his lifetime
Renowned world wide
Good defeating evil
Brings pleasure to the mind.

BASS BREWERY

Founded in 1777 by William Bass
An Empire in the making
From Barley, Hops and Mash.
2000 Barrels a year relayed
Along river Trent and Mersey Canal
To local, then Baltic trade.
In 1823 a new ale introduced
Successful for Bass Brewery
As exports he did push.
By 1823
5000 Barrels a year set sail
Brew's name tells destination
East India Pale Ale.
Midland Railway opening in 1839
Gave access to home market
For brew from Burton town.
By 1847
Sixty thousand Barrels a year
From trickle start to steady stream
Now great the flow of beer.
More Breweries have since been built
To serve the world at large
Burton-On-Trent and Britain's trade
Owes much to William Bass.

MAXWELL

He came upon us out of Hell
To seek shelter, then our wealth
Large appetite for money, lust for power
Left many naked, feeling sour.
Rich or poor, pensioner or young
Had no mercy when he stung
Important people did beguile
Arrogance and threats were his style
Gobbled up companies, newspaper owned
Fraud always on his furtive mind
Most fell for the lies he told.
His picture in the *Mirror*
Gave us all palpitations
On gold plated yacht he absconded
He died alone, out of sight
We count the cost
Big Blob of tripe.

EDINBURGH CASTLE

Scotland's fighting History, Tattoo and Scottish crown
Await the pleasure of our guests
As volcanic rock they stride
From the middle ages, through siege, pillage and gun
Against all adversity, has stood the test of time.
Standing by main entrance, proud from battles past,
Robert the Bruce, with Wallace the Braveheart.
Mary Queen of Scots gave birth here to her son
She lost her head to the axe but son would King become.
In Highland or Lowland dress, our warriors have charged
Scattered far and wide they lay to honour freedoms cause
Their memories are revered in our museum books
Read with thoughts of brave men, we cherish as you look.
Mons Meg our mighty cannon, weapons from ancient times
Dungeons and Palace are guarded by Garrison inside.
At one o'clock with shot and sign we give time of the day
To ships of fleet on Firth of Forth
A tradition here to stay.
From ramparts look down in awe on panoramic view
Down Princess Street, across the Firth of Forth
The Pipes and Drums call you.

THE GUARDIANS
OF HEATHER AND GLEN

Scotland has many heroes, of three we are most proud,
Helped keep us free from foreign yoke
For centuries in time.
William Wallace, legend in film, Braveheart
Organized resistance, of commoners took charge.
In year 1297 near Stirling made his stand
On narrow bridge above water deep
The English fled or died.
He captured Stirling Castle, ravaged England's north
Lack of resources brought him to a stop.
In year 1305 was hanged as a traitor to English king
Disembowelled, beheaded, quartered, a martyr to his kin.
Robert the Bruce, our famous Scottish king
Fought the English army in year 1314.
At Bannockburn on marshy ground
Ensnared England's mounted knights
As horses hooves bogged down
The Clans attacked with might.
Rob Roy of Clan Macgregor, our Scottish Robin Hood,
His name lives on in folklore, staunch patriot he stood.
As Jacobite supporter by English was outlawed.
In year 1731, died peacefully as he slept.
On festive occasions we remember them in song
'OH FLOWER OF SCOTLAND'.
Their memories live on.

NESSIE

From murky depths of Loch Ness
Like large upturned boat
Nessie rises to amaze
And startle honest folk.
People come from round the globe
Hoping to catch a glimpse
Of Nessie on the surface
Before she slowly sinks.
Men hunt her with Solar
The darkest fathoms scan
But Loch holds fast the secret
Of Nessie and her clan.

RABBIE BURNS

Oor great Scottish poet
As mony of his kin
He liked the lassies
Nae doot of that
As they flirted
Wi the hem.
It's been said
He fondled mony
In Tavern
And But and Ben.
His wis the spirit
Tae live his life
As only he saw fit
Withoot the dread
Of whit wis waitin
For him
Beyond the grave.

BURNS NIGHT

Wi tatties, Neeps and Haggis
And mony a wee dram
We celebrate his memory
The Bard of oor Hameland.

THE BEGINNING

To the sea of life
From virgin stream
In innocence awake
To love's sweet theme,
The touch, a feel of warm caress
Exciting scent of other flesh,
Soft mouth on taste buds
A yearning rung
Emotions entwined, journey begun.
From embrace to climax throe
A life in balance swims to grow.

CONCEIVED

Out of the sanctuary of the womb
Nourished to be born in tune.
You search through life
Till death stare
The cord of unity
You found there.
Just before about to die
Your whole existence flashes by,
If span lived in good mode
A womb like warmth on you bestowed.

GROWTH

From little acorn
To mighty oak
The brain you feed
A mind to coax.
From small beginnings
Comes a phrase
That in memory stays.
Take in the bad vibes
Digest, Discard
Then from the good
A feast is had.

INNOCENCE

No subconscious twisting of the limbs
As with guilt the body rings
No tossing, turning to and fro
With troubles in the brain's fast flow.
You lie at peace unaware
Warm and cosy in your cot.
Poverty or wealth don't bother you
No ugly thoughts in your mind
Or worry just to survive.
For you are new to life's ways
In limbo from
The thoughts that plague.

1941 – THE TAWSE

In Scottish schools
It reigned supreme
For many generations
Of leather made
Two inches wide
The hand and wrist
With might did find.
Cut into strips
Giving much pain
Red weals of discipline
Was tawse's aim.
Five years old
A tiny mite
In front of class
He stood
For peeing against
The wall of school
Was now about
To pay in full.
The Tawse came down
Six times in all
Made hand swell
He wanted to bawl
But with his pride
Now at stake
Unflinching he stared ahead.
The tawse was
Law and order

Teachers with parents
In control
Of offsprings who
Stepped out of line
Made to do
As they were told.

THE AULD SHANK

It stands by
Loch Leven road
Many a tale
Pub: walls been told
From days of sawdust
And spittoon
When clothed capped miners
Drank till full.
Blue scars on faces
Stood out stark
From coal dust in cuts
As seam they hacked.
Pick and shovelling
Ten hour shifts
'Auld shank' their pleasure
From back breaking pit.
Pitch and toss
Watch pennies spin
As with mates
Joke and drink.
Whisky glass turned
Upside down
A challenge to a fight,
Only fists they did use
Their code of honour
Now grimy news.

THE PIT PIECE

It was no morsel of great taste
Stale bread with jam that tasted sooty.
But it had been when your heroes go
Down the coalmine far below.
The miners saved some for the kids
On Mary pit road at end of shift.
Pit siren wails in still of night
You wake up mam who dresses quick.
With her you stand at the pit head
As cage brings up deformed and dead.
No longer will you see dad grin
Holding out pit piece
In vacuumed tin.
On Lochore meadows now made for pleasure
Ghost with pit piece below for ever.

JAM JARS OF HOT TEA

Coal fire burning bright
Tin bath on fire rug ready
Waiting on Gran's miner sons
His uncles Sam and Eddie.
On black leaded hob
Two jam jars of hot tea
Best china kept for Sundays
That's how it used to be.
Who would win the race
To step into tin bath
Then with a grin
Leave water black
The loser's lot to have,
Uncle Sam's the winner
Gulps his jar of tea
To clear his throat of coal dust
Gargles with great glee.
Pit siren gives its mournful wail
Disaster down below,
Granny's face goes tense and white
Somehow the worst she knows.
Eddie's jar of tea shudders on the hob
Then with a crash falls to the floor
With no one near to touch.
Sam looking dejected
Wearily gets dressed
Pit clothes he puts in bath to soak

He knows where Eddie rests.
All have now departed earth
Somewhere they wait for him
On Granny's hob he knows there sits
His jam jar of hot tea.

D-DAY
JUNE 6TH 1944

From British Isles this day would die
Proud young men for freedoms cry.
To vanquish tyranny of Nazi Heil,
As Europe it raped, enslaved, defiled.
The allies did Germans much confuse
In dummy bases, machines and news.
With backup strong the Nazis scanned
Beaches not in battle plan.
Then allied forces made history
Crossed English Channel on this, D-Day.

The sky was filled with drone and shapes
Of airborne armada with much at stake,
Towing large gliders filled with men
To glide inland, disrupt, defend.
The sea alive with ships enmasse
Some floating harbours towing aft
A fuel line under sea
Would sustain attack into Germany.
From Normandy beaches troops stormed ashore
To fight the Nazis to poisoned core.

Many years have gone on by
Their deeds of valour will never die.
The suffering for us was not in vain
We bow our heads, freedom still reigns.
Remember we will the debt that's due
Till unto death we join with you.

GORBALS MAN

Born in a Glasgow slum
A life in squalor had begun
One toilet on the tenement stair
All who lived there
Had to share.
Foul smelling, overflowing loo
A nightmare for all who used.
Over-crowded, six to a bed
Lucky if you owned a chair
In the days when jobs did not exist.
Each tenement had its tribal gang
Lives were ruled by Razor scars
Or head butt known as Glasgow kiss
So not much difference from then to this.
In this environment humans survived
The blood line not to be denied.
For this mockery of a life
Men for country, gave lives and limbs.

MAN IN STITCHES

Harold Parslow take a bow
Stitched all over, inside and out
Shrapnel wounds to nose and head
One toe taken clean from flesh.
Surgeon's knife at stomach aimed
Nevus giving so much pain,
Gallbladder removed, in despair
Hospital becoming a care home.
A battle with cancer tumour
Saw him near the end of tether
Blood clots gave the heart a jolt
Then double hernia took hold.
Hip joints now has had replaced
Profanity utters as patience strays.
Could I be as strong I wonder.
A bookworm with standards high
An education for you and I.

V.E. DAY

Church bells rang
Gave out the news
Victory was ours
In World War Two.
The nation poured
Into the streets
With hugs and cheers
Tears of relief.
At last we're free
Of Nazi Heil
Bombs, bullets, torture
Gas chambers file.
Streets were turned
From drab to gay
With Union Jacks
On proud display.
Tables laid out
For a feast
Ration books emptied
Supplied the eats.
Okie koky, Lambeth walk
Singing, dancing as rejoiced
Blackout over, street lights on,
Starting of
A bright new dawn.
The world owes much
To bulldog breed
We gave our best
Freedom to keep.

1945
REMEMBER WHEN

Worn out shoes scratched up knees
A jumper threadbare, stiff in cuff
From umpteen usage for nose and such,
The bite of strap from teachers strict
Red weals of discipline in its grip.
Rupert bear in daily paper
Teaching of a different nature.
Open fields and hills to roam
Safe to let loose on your own,
Following the baker's horse
Garden manure not to be lost,
Cart load of coal dumped in the street
Stacked in back yard before you eat.
Pit clothes soaking in tin bath
After Ma had washed Dad's back.
Stale jam sandwich returned from pit
Eaten with great pride
A penny for the pictures
Which were all black and white.
Cleaning fire range with black lead
A must also the front door step.
Queued five hours for bread and meat
Dropped under a bus
Took home in fright now tyred to mush.
Sweets were rationed a quarter a week
But I still have all my front teeth.
A bonfire large to celebrate
Returning heroes from the war
In shadowy fringe I kissed and touched
Young Jenny I adored.

FACTORY, LOVES AND MARRIAGES

FACTORY FLOOR

Sign language used
To communicate
Ears plugged against
Noise of machines.
His tee shirt smells
Of oil and sweat
Feet ache from contact
With concrete,
From dust and fumes
Eye whites are red
For all his effort
And wage cuts
To cheap imports
His job is lost.
Now with clear white
Eyeball surrounds
He stands in dole queue
For a handout.

FACTORY HARASSMENT

She is a wages clerk
Dress style is demure
To cut down on harassment
As she walks the factory floor.
Daily runs the gauntlet
Of whistler, groper, pinch
And arm over shoulder
Touching awkward bits.
Now don't get me wrong
Our Jan is no prude
Will sit on knee
Smudge your lips
In Christmas party mood.
But our Clive has her puzzled
He uses different ploy
No way would he
Touch her thigh
Or other ways annoy.
He is the answer
To many a maiden's prayer
A bachelor with brand new car
And a boat on Windermere.
He also keeps the budgies
Jan has had invite
To coo with him
Stroke little breasts
In aviary one night.
He calls her his little virgin
I think he's overkeen
She soon will be a grandma
But Clive he has a dream.
To see his favourite henbird
Rocking as she steers
While he puts away the anchor
On a lake called Windermere.

WARNING!

A lowering of the tone. The next tale is rather disgusting, although basically true. If you are of a squeamish nature and not a nosey person, avoid reading.

THE BOGEY MAN

With finger deep in nostril hair
He rucks out muck trapped up there
So he can breathe, in the fresh air
Then decorates loo wall with care.
His hobby through factory gossip spread
Now even reached the Internet.
Now has a fan club world wide
They say great works of art abound,
Confessions then came of uncovered sneezes
And hanky inspections in public places,
If you should wake in the night
With stuffed up nose and a picking sound
Do not worry it's a nightmare, of E-Mails
And the thoughts you share
No way would you touch nasal fare.
Loo walls tell us in great detail
Of ignorance in which we dwell.

LOVES

LOVE'S TANGLED WEB

Compassion is love
To those with cross to bear
For others in oblivion
With dreams blank as they stare.
Relating love to close at heart
Great anguish felt when world depart
Consumes the mind to ultimate low
Until the wake of departed soul.
Love of power split a nation
White House was therapeutic patient.
Love also plays the heartstrings
Gives tears and joy in uneven tread.
Must have, don't count the cost
A sting in tail of love ill bought
A love child brings new meaning
With each genetic seed
For some blessing created
To others life-long grief.
Love can also turn to hate
Fill with vengeful thoughts
When love is dealt a double cross.
To a one night stand
Word can be stretched
Or mile high club in a tight head.
But there is a love that's total
In body, mind and soul
Lifelong commitment
To make two become whole.

APHRODITE

Hair caught in moonlight
Framed the face in gold
Lips full with sensuous line
Bone structure in lean mode.
As from sea she arose
Full beauty came to view.
Breast glistening in water bead
Trickled down navel
The sea to feed
Body supple, limbs long
Naked as the goddess born
Moulded in such perfect shape.
No apple needed
Man to bait.

TEENY LOVE

My eyes are streaming
From tears are stung
You've left me for
Another one.
Mary Bell is her name
You told her lies
To stake a claim.
Said that I cheated on you
With a boy called Johnny Blue.
She knows of our foreplay
Each secret you gave away.
Her claws are out
With tongue so sharp
Tells all and sundry
Of our romps in the park.
I walk down town
To cat calls
'She pulled the plug on Bobby Hall'
In front of buddies
You feel real big
Exaggerate what I did
People think I'm no good at all
'She pulled the plug on Bobby Hall'

IN TUNE

With friendly smile caught my eye
Long of limb, slim with style
We both had known depths of despair
Which in this life is not rare.
Experiences from the past
Teaches tongue to be not rash
Now both give as united one
All life's fruits under the sun
If selfish in attitude
Coupling of flesh like tainted food
Two natures in human made
Some born to give, the others take.

STEADY DATE

It's Saturday night
I meet my date
With a hug
She sure looks great,
We walk along street
Dressed in style.
A bottle of expensive wine
In top restaurant as we unwind
Her striking good looks
Turn heads with admiring stares.
Don't give a damn cause I'm her man
We hit the high spots while we can.
On we go to Casino
Play the tables, see a show
My wallet now feels the chill.
Don't give a damn cause I'm your man
We hit the high spots while we can.
Back in dingy basement flat
Reality comes back to haunt.
But you respond to my touch
As my hands gently roam
Till we're in a state of lust.
Don't give a damn cause I'm your man
We hit the high spot when we can.

OPPOSITES

Life is a turning of sun to rain
Joy and laughter to tears of grief
This is how it's meant to be
Two extremes like day and night.
Life is a turning of kind to cruel
The honest and the criminal mind
This is how it's meant to be
Two extremes like dawn and dusk.
Life is a turning to penetrate
Other to give birth from mate
This is how it's meant to be
Two extremes in harmony.
Life is a turning young to old
Two extremes who hands now hold
This is how it's meant to be
Till walk as one in eternity.

ALL SAINTS CHURCH

Our church has stood
The test of time
From thirteenth century
Committed are its members
To peace and harmony.
The Reverend Michael Drew
Is a stout Cornishman
A trusted willing listener
To all his faithful flock,
Ben Cummings the Church Warden
Was born in Dundee,
Essex girl, Lesley Campion
Shares duties if need be.
Bell Master Alan Cattell
Three bells he rings with zest
In call to all who worship
The name of God to bless.
Marion Bancroft is our Organist
She gives with subtle skill
A melody in setting
With Cross upon a hill.
Christianity has flourished here
Since the year 1043.

WEDDING BLESSING

At Humberstone church
You took your vows
To stay faithful
Throughout your lives
Love and joy
Are easily claimed
But tolerance needed
To keep the same.
Do not belittle
The one you chose
In front of friends
Relations or foes,
Love and companionship
Can last life through
If indiscretions forgiven
Between you two
And not aired for public view.

THE HONEYMOON

From exchange of rings
Vows now bind, two in trust.
After all the celebrations
From the world they retreat,
In embrace of tenderness
To cries of delight
As passion explodes.
The flowing of love stream
Sighs of content
All of the senses
Now truly spent.
Holding each other
In warm embrace
As sleep encroaches
On each other's gaze.

KIDS

You cannot tell what you have got
From angel face to ugly mop.
Will innocence stay or recede
As in mean streets their footsteps lead.
Will they get into booze and smokes
Or on the drugs minds grow remote.
Will they go bent, rampage and steal
Or stay as hoped on honest trail.
It all is in the hands of fate
Parenthood for all cannot be great.

CHALK AND CHEESE

Girl head shaven, boy in curl
Are the sexes in a twirl.
Chalk is moody, sometimes crude
Cheese thinks it smells of all things good.
One gets car sick, nerves on twitch
The other niggles till you itch.
Chalk sleepwalks then wakes with ease
You turn red to get up Cheese.
One is tidy to a fault
To other's mess there is no halt.
Chalk helps around the house
Cheese runs off to trap a mouse.
One has music in the ear
The other's potential none too clear.
Cheese into karate big
Chalk-game of poddy does not dig.
One thing in common it is true
Hate being told what to do.
Like cat and dog they will fight
But don't like school mates one to spite.
Chalk keeps busy, writes real good
But always thinks is understood.
Cheese tries hard but cannot spell
Also has no sense of smell.
If you have a chalk and cheese
We know like us you cannot please.

WHO IS TO BLAME?

Some kids for exercise
Fetch nightly takeaways
Sit on fat little bums
Guzzling food and drink.
It's stumpy or long legs
Dangling at all angles
From beds, settees and chairs.
Watch parents work
At the daily chores
Offer them no help,
Giggle as they watch Dad
In garden with back bent.
They think that washing up
Is Mummy's job for sure
Will turn deaf not move their feet
As she hoovers the floor.
They never offer help
To carry from the car
Shopping for their greedy tums
As far as the front door.
When asked to clean their rooms
Or pick up scattered clothes
Treat all to puzzled look.
They won't know what it's about
Till they have their own babes
And realize how hard it is
To be a parent slave.

MANIX THE DOG

This dog was extra special
To owner and his son
It fetched their papers
Shoes and socks
Odd errand it would run.
On visits to the village pub
Would partake of the drink
From large ashtray
'Specially kept for him.
On its demise from old age
New dog was bought
To take his place.
It liked to chew on everything
From slippers to a wedding ring
What this mutt did for fun
Brought misery to owner
And his son.
Until one day it went too far
Fridge Freezer cable
Gnawed and chewed.
If you want a mutt that's electrified
With frizzled coat and jerky run
Just knock the door
Of Tom the son.

MONDAY MORNING

You may well know the feeling
As you sit on edge of bed
Stomach aches from Sunday lunch
Late drinks swim in thick head.
You stagger to the bathroom
Teeth are not in glass
Some prankster's stuck them grinning
In the soap bar by the bath.
Groomed and dressed minus one sock
You make it down to hall
A jobby waits by doggy's side
Lost sock lies by its ball.
The car won't start, train's running late
For bus the rush hour queue
Impatiently awaiting
The boss with Monday blues.
You get your cards, yes it's the sack
Whatever will you do
The car is due its M.O.T.
Arrears in mortgage new.
Back on the street you slide into
A pavement takeaway
You think your ankle's broken
In curried chips with tray.
Twenty pounds they bill you
For ambulance and crew
To sit six hours in casualty
Wondering why you.
No welcome home from offsprings

Wife or family pets
All eyes and ears are riveted
On the television set
Yes you're right you've guessed it
It's a Coronation Street repeat
Curly's trying to fathom
A barmaid who is petite
She simpers hot air in his ear
But suffers from cold feet.
You crawl upstairs in great distress
Slide between the sheets
Monday's almost over
It swept you off your feet.

THE SANCTUARY

Locked in seclusion
Slowly sinking into
Steamy haze.
The stress of the day
Left in your wake.
Time to abandon your mind
To warm relaxation
Of aching limbs,
Till fantasy takes over
From reality.
Through semi-conscious state
The muffled sound of voices
Rising to a crescendo.
An insistent hammering
Hits your brain,
'You've been in there for ages,
Let us in before we burst'
With pull of plug
Your dreams run away.
Quickly dried and robed
To face sullen, flushed faces,
Sanctuary invaded once more.

ONE OF MANY

Eyes sunk deep in sockets
Mouth now ragged grin
Ears rearranged all twisted
like cauliflowers in spring.
Neck sunk in threadbare shoulders
supports lopsided head
One arm hangs from elbow
by a strip of thread.
Leg missing after tantrums
on a summer's day
Because of sudden downpour
no one went out to play.
Stomach once rotund
now cuddled flat.
Loved as someone special
A comfort in the dark.
Lost to puberty and marriage
till voice shouts from upstairs
'Guess what I've found Mum.
It's my old TEDDY BEAR'

ANNIVERSARY

Around candlelit table
The mood is bright
As another year
Our union celebrate
For you my spouse
My love is great.
We mellow as older grow
With trouble and strife
Upbringing behind
No bitterness
Or axe to grind
The two of us
Are closer bound.

WYNN

Her head she raised
To meet my eyes
I lost my tongue
Then stuttered some.
From that first look
With feelings new
Romance by chance
Out of the blue.
As years go by
Though eyes grow dim
Just raises head
My heart to win.

MIND BENDER

Two days in a drunken state
He staggers home
To face her wrath
Of his limbs he's lost control
Body in constant rock and fall
With vision blurred
His mind in space
Into the gutter he has sunk.
Finally gets carried home
To face the fury
Of her indoors.
Never again he says when sober.
On pay day states
With conviction
Just one more before
I hit the road.

THE VASECTOMY

His doctor enquired
Why he wanted this done.
His pension was already stretched
Keeping a young wife,
Lying naked from waist down
He tried not to cringe
As surgeon in gown and mask
Said he would not feel a thing.
It made this man realise
The embarrassment and pain
That women in life go through.
Ice cold antiseptic
Rubbed on to shaven scrotum
Needle then injected
Till private parts were frozen.
Incisions under manhood
Production tubes then snipped
Removal of two portions
So sperm can't jump the bridge.
Ends of tubes sealed skilfully
Incisions stitched and dressed.
His young wife all excited
Nearly crashed the car
As he sat terror stricken
Feeling sore and blue.
Although it took nine months
For the sperm all clear
He now shares marriage bed
Smiling from ear to ear.

JOCK REGRETS

Sorry to say 'Big Yin'
Can't be with you tonight
To celebrate your forty-second
With whisky and a pint
I would have sent my partner
But she is rather shy
Besides she has to nurse me
Horizontal I must lie.
'*Full moon*' will be jumping
Throbbing to the beat
The banquet as usual
Quality to feast.
With spirits, beer a flowing
No sign of any speed
I know for all it's going to be
A great big Richies bash.
Had four o'clock appointment
With surgeon name of Roger
On shaven scrotum he made incisions
Just below my Podger.
Production tubes snipped expertly
Parts removed he showed to me,
Ends sealed up, tucked away
Stitched and dressed by tea.
Down below blackish hue
Feeling rather numb
The things we do for womenfolk
To make their lives more fun.
A hundred pounds it cost me

It will be worth it though
My pension book will now be safe
No child from it will grow.
Podger isn't pleased with me
He looks a sorry sight
I'm sure he thinks I did it
Out of bloody-minded spite.
Will see you very soon
When I am on the mend
And Podger with all worry shed
Is proud of me again.

LOVE AND HATE

My life has been a mixture
Of best and worst in you,
From jealousy and spite
To love and joy we knew.
There never seems to be
An in-between to it,
No understanding of the feelings
That make us so exist.
But love and hate
Don't give a damn
For meaning as they flow
As they are things
Beyond the grasp
Of we who they control.

WHITER THAN WHITE

Dressed in white
From head to toe
I waited humiliated
Outside of church
For husband to be
To show up.
But you did a runner
That very day
With my sister Marjorie.
A more lazy bitch
Would be hard to find
She lies in bed
Until well past noon
And don't expect
A meal that's cooked.
Will make your life
A living hell
With credit cards
And shopping bills.
She also likes
To flirt a bit
So beware when you
Are on night shift.
Now it's all over
Between ourselves,
Apart from maintenance
In two months that's due
I will share a secret
That will bother you.
From your twin brother
Him called Joe,
The bulge in wedding
dress did show.

NIGHTMARE

Whatever happened to young love
Lying there like clotted cream
Matted hair, baggy eyes
Roaring out snoring sighs
Mouth parted in a leering grin,
Chins quivering in their folds.
What was once tight to the ribs
Now wobbles about as it sees fit.
A tear rolls out of partner's eye
Thinking of days gone by
When both of them
Were all the rage.

LADY LUCK

You rolled the dice, took a chance
With Lady Luck by your side
In gambling fever all lit up,
Soon you became a high flier
The game of chance only desire.
For two years all went your way
Then suddenly she deserted you
The chips were down, your life askew.
From a high to a low
A winner rich to loser make
For Lady Luck has been bought
By great deceiver, Big Jackpot.

MUTTON DRESSED AS LAMB

He sensed from the beginning
That as the years went by
Make up on face would turn to cake
She'll end up looking like a tart.
On shopping trips in town
Embarrassed he lagged behind.
She totters along the street
In six inch stiletto heels,
Skirt half way up her bum
Knickers flashing, ladders run
A teenage tart of seventy one.
One day after a trip to town
In a soothing voice he said,
I think you would look better
If you dressed more like your age'
She eyed him in stunned silence
Could not believe her ears
Who the hell did he think he was
Telling her what she should wear.
'Mutton dressed as lamb is it
That's what you think of me'
Her cigarette dropped
From bright red gash
Into his cup of tea.
My old ma God bless her
Told me I would regret
The day you had your wicked way
And wedding day was set.
I could have had the pick

Of all the men I knew
I must have been off my head
To finish up with you.
She said you'd use me as a slave
And have your way in bed,
She was half right
But I shut up tight
In spare room you've slept and read.
You're nothing but a windbag
Fed up I am with you
While I'm at the Bingo
Go flush yourself down loo.

BINGO

House she shouts
In nervous voice
The fat lady sitting
At table three.
As card is checked
A buzz of noise
Fills the hall.
Lucky bitch has won again
I only wanted number ten.
Three full houses in a row
It must be a fiddle
With caller Joe.
I saw him leave her house last night
Looking drained and deadly white.
I reckon she'd hit
The Jackpot there
They say he makes love like a bear.
Sudden silence fills the hall
It's eyes down for the big game.
Housewives love this
Game of chance
As they dream of Jackpot
Who knows, maybe romance.

LOVE UNTANGLED

Its enormity of feeling
Can reach the darkest depths
Give lift to great joy
As eyes on one are set.
It releases great tenderness
In caress or holding hands
But also sends you spiralling down
To jealous rage and taunts.
Its many forms made
From instincts deep in us
From love of close family
To unseen face above.
Nature in its seasons
Steamy breath and fluffy snow
Spring's cherry tree blossom
With shades of green in the hedgerow.
Summer's golden harvest
To mellow shades of autumn's fall.
Love of your country
Or favourite sporting team
Pet animal or bird in gilded cage.
It rules us from birth of babe
To senile in decay.

POPULAR SPORTS & ENTERTAINMENT

A WORRIED FAN

Whatever happened to the days
When footballers and fans were pals
Played the game for peanuts
With a seat for friend in Stand.
They didn't lead the jet set life
Or live on Caviar
Just fish and chips
On match day nights
Or a pint with fans in bar.
Some may have had five bellies
But they kept a low profile
Boots that protected ankles
With solid toe for power,
A ball of heavy leather
When wet it weighed a ton
Could turn the head to jelly
If not timed right on a run.
Fans not segregated, often shared a flask
Kids were handed over heads
Down front for view of park.
Come back Stanley Mathews,
Busby, Ramsey, Shanks.
And all who played the game
Wore their club shirts with pride.

MANCHESTER UNITED

More than a football club
A family of a kind
At Stretford end on Trafford road
On match days we are found.
From glory of the Busby Babes
Ill fated in their role
Whose standards are now legend
To attain them is the goal.
Just one decade from Munich
Bobby Charlton at the fore
The European Cup held high
By George Best and Denis Law.
We've not had many lean times
As new babes were waiting
With Giggs, Scholes and Beckham
In dream team to take part.
We also had French maestro
Oh! Oh! Cantona
Master of his craft.
Let's hope that future players
Who trophy cabinets fill
Don't let self ego and avarice
Tarnish the memories
Of our club's great legends.

MILLWALL – THE NEW DEN

New Den is more comfy now
For visitors and fans
The lions happy in new home
Contented and well fed.
Hooligans who wrecked our dreams
And our resources drained
Steps taken to get rid of them
Will benefit our name.
We give a pledge to our true fans
Who follow, cause no grief
Promotion to a higher goal
We will try our best to reach.

A TRIBUTE TO BOBBY MOORE

At Wembley Stadium he held it high
He won the World Football Cup
With the team that he led
For the Nation brought success
Sweat and tears into extra time
Till in favour was scoreline.
He wiped his hands
On a cover of velvet
Before the Queen
Her hand did offer
A thoughtful act
In his time of glory.
He played for West Ham at seventeen
A talent of which you only dream
Slim and fair with youthful zeal
A football brain above the rest
With skill and grace a game dictated
Leaving spectators in a trance.
In England shirt at twenty three
His prowess all the world did see
The memory of this shy man's name
Will live forever in the game.

GARY LINEKAR

A city of Leicester favourite son
Soccer ambassador second to none,
Striker with the magic touch
Scored goals galore with little fuss.
With Leicester, Everton, Tottenham
His skill and instinct thrilled the fans.
Transferred to Europe's sunny Spain
At Barcelona spread his fame.
Top scorer in the world cup
Won golden boot an England plus.
Though sometimes kicked black and blue
Retaliation we never viewed.
In Leicester Market his family trades
No prouder kin has one man made.

PLAY

Forwards with tiger in their blood
Strain each sinew in dry or mud.
Ears wrapped in bandage thick
So roughed up from scrummage hit.
Ram head on to get the heel
To force opponents down the field,
Steam arises as from wet dung
When in wet weather they do scrum,
As tempers blow in the maul
Referee calls Captains, to lecture all.
Up and under, charge as one
From penalty ball must be won
Scrum Half's shoulder thumps into thigh
Prop Forward to the ground he scythes.
From loose ball 'Stand Off' drop kicks
Scores over bar, defence unknit.
Forwards in line out, clutch or tap
To feed three quarters with pass back
Ball from Centre to the Wing.
With flying dive a try to win,
At Rugby school, man ran with ball
Now world his stage to enthral.

RUGBY IN UNION (INTERNATIONALS)

National pride in afternoon
The stadiums fill with anthem's tune
Proud England stand, red rose on white
As 'God Save the Queen' the crowd sing out,
Kiwis with nostrils all aflare
Chant the 'haka,' leap in air
'Land of My Fathers' from massed Welsh choir
Emotions for country does inspire.
In shirts of gold Aussies composed
Feel victory is their abode.
A cheer erupts from Irish and French
Fast running game supporters sense.
Before the start of Murrayfield show
'Flower of Scotland,' chills the foe.
Flags and Mascots join Shamrocks, Leeks
From all nations who union teach.
Argentina and Italy
Now with us mix.

RUGBY – CELTIC STYLE

Proud in the colour
Of Emerald Isle green
Win or lose
We try our best
For our country
And our kin.
In nineteen ninety three
A memorable win
Over a strong England side
To take the triple
rugby crown.
It took us over
sixty long years
To repeat a grand slam win
With final match
Away from home
Against a great Welsh team
Who failed in last minute
With penalty kick to win.
With nerves in shreds
All Ireland rejoiced
Of six nations
Now top team.

A scenic beauty is our land
With Blarney Stone
To make a wish
And greens of every hue.
Famine spread the Irish gene

Around the World
And to the American dream.
Our kin return to reminisce
Of rugby and six nations best.

GOLF'S EFFEN-HELL

His name resounds
From Tee to Tee
In the rough
And out of bounds
Where he hides in wait
On golf balls to pounce,
He is a Ferret of a man
Over eager to poach balls
A permanent lump on head
stands out.
Instead of the warning
Shout of fore
Effen-Hell is shouted
More and more.
He thinks all golfers
Are quite mad
As with wild swings
In bunkers land.
When ball rolls back
From bunker tip
Effen-Hell on golfers
Minds and lips.
Spectators also shout his name
From the stands and fairways.
For all budding White Sharks,
Montys, Faldos and Tiger Woods
Effen-Hell awaits
When swing not good.

TENNIS – WIMBLEDON

From Henman Hill
To Centre Court
We watch the power
And subtle skills
From players of both
Sexes
At top of their sport.
Great champions and characters
In male game have appeared
But one stands out
For great play and utterances
Through games he played, delayed.
'You cannot be serious'
He would declare
To the Umpire sat
High up in chair.
His tantrums were
In sharp contrast
To the pomp and ceremony
Wimbledon creates.

The female game
Brings glamour
With pretty maids
Dressed to thrill
Admirers of both sexes.
But then a few
To spectator's dismay
Grunt, shout and scream
Each shot they play.

It's time to make an exit
For strawberries and cream
And reflect on all forms
Of gamesmanship in sport.

SNOOKER PROFESSIONALS

With dedication and practice
From an early age
Until become professionals
And take the world stage.
Their composure is impressive
To say the very least
As crowd in auditorium
Watch their every move
And spectators in armchairs
Take television view.
Some can be irritating
Their patience
Strains your nerves
As they study every angle
Before a shot is played.
Others more flamboyant
Move around the table
With just a glancing look
To pot a red ball
Leave angle on the black,
Balls now well placed for
Maximum jackpot.
Respect is two-fold
In this sport
As player bends
The ball to cue
Silence spreads in the hall
And players act as gentlemen
A credit to their temperaments.

HORSE RACING

The King of Sports it is often called, with fans from every walk of life. Through horse racing fraternity dedication and endeavour are clearly seen. To the flat races and over the jumps crowds flock, for an awakening of their senses. The Grand National with large field of mounts brings out emotions of all kinds. From ecstasy of winning punters, owner and stable, to grief for horse that stumbled, fell and trampled jockey on the ground. A jockey named Richard Dunwoody was a past winner of the race, three times also became a cropper at famous jump called Becher's Brook, as he went flying from his steed. Under thunder of hooves he survived, now smiles as recalls the adrenaline drive. In sharp contrast is Ascot races on Ladies' Day with its delightful fashion parade. With hats of all shapes and size, with dresses to match on proud display. Champagne by the magnum drunk, day to relax and have some fun. It's the Queen of England's favourite sport. Not many winners does she have, apart from steeds who seat her Coldstream Guards.

COOL HEAD COLE

Not for him a stroll from pub bar, to place wagers at assorted odds on each way bets, or a straight win on dodgy hooves and temperaments. He never has a two or three spread flutter on major races like many others. Or has a bet on a horses name, coincidence he treats with disdain. To him a jockey is as good as horse he whips past winning post. From form book, stable and owner chatter he makes his living as a professional backer. 'Cool Head Cole' has earned his name by years of studying the betting game. Now well groomed and distinguished mixes in top racing circles. His fame has spread from course to course, looked on with awe and admiration. As horses parade before the start only odds on favourite attracts his gaze. His steely eyes don't miss a thing, of condition or the mood that the horse is in. Around twenty bets he has a year to keep him in a lifestyle of great cheer. 'Cool Head Cole's a punter's dream, *his* odds on favourites always win.

THE TIPSY FISHERMAN

As hosts of our quaint Inn
We extend a hearty welcome
Relax at leisure with a beer
In our friendly atmosphere.
Add to these ancient walls
The many fishy tales been told,
Fishing for the largest Carp
Sees Dave up sometimes
While it's still dark,
Our Siamese cat belongs to Sue
Will purr content
Within your view.
Of cat and fish chat without risk
As sup the ale or taste of dish
We wish to serve in manner true
With joy again at seeing you.
Dave's homemade bait
Awaits your pleasure
Any time you come to fish
And enjoy the banter
With a drink.

AT ONE WITH NATURE

In the still
Of moonlight scene
On river bank
No troubles dream.
Alone in tranquillity
I cast my line
On shimmering lay.
A quiver of rod
With wits we fight
Till I have captive
Large silver trout.
The gentle freeing
Off the hook
Swim back my beauty
To your roots.
Great sense of freedom
You bring to me
This captive to
A clock for fee.

WORLD SERIES

Super Bowl final
A dream come true
Our team is there
To win on cue.
Helmeted, padded
To run and block
Opposition at all points stop.
Back and forth
The game does sway
Scores level
Into final play.
From mighty throw
Touch down run
Hard victory
Has been won.
We coaches, cheer leaders
Supporters all
Will treasure in memory
Our Super Bowl.

ICE DANCE

They speed over ice with skill and grace
Minds to delight, eyes to amaze.
Samba, rumba, rock and roll
Artistic impression from them flow.
With technical merit to each pair
As modern or classic dance,
Spinning, jumping, somersaults
Crowd willing them be best of all.
In glittering costumes skim the ice
Two in harmony with romantic bite.
To the Torvil and the Deane
We look on you with high esteem.

SIMPLY THE BEST

I have a great admiration for the singer Tina Turner. Not only as an entertainer but for all she has had to endure in her life. I also found out that the lady has a great sense of humour after handing in the following verse at her Murrayfield Rugby Stadium concert some years ago. Two months later I received a signed photo from her home in Switzerland as a thank you.

TINA TURNER

At home on stage
Fronting big band
Giving of the fever
In a one night stand
Tina-Turn-On
Singing for my supper
Giving of the beat
To sister and brother,
With high-lighted hair
Topping coffee coloured skin
Dressed to make
The fellas think of sin.
Bouncing and stomping
Hitting high note
High heels help
Keep the beat afloat
Slow down now
To a romantic low
Reach the heart strings
Of those below.
In spotlight glare
Feel all lit up
Drinking deep
From adrenalin cup
Crowd a clapping
Shouting my name
Nothing more exciting
Than spotlight frame,
Giving of the fever
All the rage
Love singing out
To half my age.

DISCO MAN

It's Saturday night, he is smartly groomed, in a colourful shirt, sprayed with perfume. Now he's John Travolta in his mind, with confidence he hits the town, to meet up with a gang of mates. In the Market Tavern, O'gradys and O'neils they chat and drink, with the music get into party mood. With glazed eyes and now loose tongues to a Nightclub stagger on.

From Nightclub bar to Disco sound, for Disco Man weekends' highlight. He struts on to the centre of the floor, like a Peacock Matador. In among the dolled up chicks, Disco Man gets his kicks, eyes up all around and favours them with body scan. The stage vibrates as band get into full swing and Funky male singer hits a high note late. Disco Man has picked a chick he thinks he can chat up real quick. As he closes in on her he Flips, Flaps with his Wings and comes on heavy with his Limbs. As his body he gyrates, manoeuvres her into spotlight front of stage. Now his ego is out of control he decides to steal a kiss or two. He hits the floor, as in a rage, chicks man Funky jumps from stage. From Bouncers' arms to taxi groans, but grins to himself on the ride home. With a black eye and two broken ribs, just another night out for a modern Brit.

ROCKIN' ROLLIN' DUMPLING

A champion dancer
In his prime
When he was once
Slim and fit
Now nearing seventy
More than rotund
Sits in pub chair
Relaxing tum.
When music plays
Taps floor with toes
And to the beat
His body sways.
When he gets up
To buy a round
Vibrates his body
Wiggles the bum
And to barmaid
Love song is sung.
Sarcastic comments
About him are made
And his large food
With drink intake,
He shrugs them off
With inward smile
Of one thing he's sure
From physical
And mental stress
Most of them
Will die the death,

As long as he
Can tap his feet
And move in harmony
With the beat
No stressful thoughts
In him will reach.

WHAT THE HELL YOU DOING?

Driving in the fast lane
To another gig
Band in the back
Packed in with the kit.
Wheel trim goes a flying
As a tyre goes bang
Rocking then rolling
In our old tin van.
Screech across the fast lane
At seventy miles plus
Hit the hard shoulder
In a cloud of dust.
Band in the back
Tangled with the kit
Gave him earache
With plenty of lip.
'What the hell you doing
You mad dimwit?'
Reached their venue
An hour late
Angry Hell's Angels
Not very pleased.
Everything tuned
Ready to play
A cheese and onion cob
Came winging his way,
He staggered back
Knocking all on stage
Into disarray.

Band back of stage
Tangled with the kit
Gave him earache
With plenty of lip,
'What the hell you doing
You damned half wit?'
The drunken pub crowd
Cheered out loud
Band in a tangle
Had made their night.
Band got their act together
All enjoyed the gig
Rocking and rolling
To guitar and banjo
Drum sticks hitting
A crescendo.
With Angels' escort
Revving their delight
Left the venue
with the van on tow.

DIVORCES

DIVORCE

It breaks the bond
Of all involved
As papers served
On marriage cold.
All branches of
The family tree
Axed with a finality
No longer stable
On emotion road
When shedding of
The family code.

The following letter was written by a studious, quiet, fourteen year old girl. The trauma of her parents' bitter divorce battle turned her into a Skinhead rebel.

SKINHEADS

1981. Skinheads stick together they dress about the same and like the same kind of music. They don't dress the same as their idols in groups. They wear Doc Martins, jeans, sto-press, pilot jackets, crombies, braces, fingerless gloves. They also wear their trousers so that they almost reach the top of their boots. Skinhead girls have their hair cut or shaved to a quarter of an inch, this is called a number four. The lads have a number one, shaved all over. Most of them have tattoos but only a few of the girls do. The groups talked about are Bad Manners, Anti-Nowhere League and Specials. Lots of people get into trouble but are not heard about because they're not Skinheads. Just because one dog kills a cat doesn't mean they all will. By this I mean just because someone does bad everybody shouldn't get the blame. Skinheads don't like posh things or the police. I used to think coloureds were okay till a group of them threw a bottle at me. We don't look for trouble but are prepared for it if it comes. All of the girls have their ears pierced at least twice. One of my friends has seventeen holes in one of her ears and her dad doesn't mind.

TORMENT OF THE RING

Looking back it was never meant to last
The flirtatious nature of her spirit
Was imprisoned by the band of gold
Pressed on her by pregnancy.
The childlike insistence on matrimonial tradition
Taking no heed of his limited resources,
Or her condition
Sent alarm bells ringing.
Surprisingly she had a flair for motherhood
From those precious baby stages,
Attentive, caring almost doting.
It was he who lacked in words if not deeds
The sentiments to give her
A more secure awareness of his presence.
The financial struggle to establish themselves
Bound them together.
At last free of child care
With city job carefully chosen
The opportunity for flattery and adulation
Her ego craved.
Nights out with the girls became more frequent
Home coming later, excuses more trivial,

Encouragement to socialize on his own.
Her breathless excitement, flushed face
On more than one late excursion
Reminded him of a summer evening
Wrestling playfully on flattened hay
Her thin cotton dress rucked high.
Jealousy and suspicion were now ripe
He knew he was being taken for a fool
The marriage was as good as over.
Tight lipped he refused to question
Afraid of the truth, his pride still intact.
Self doubt also festered
Would a daily show of adoration
With a weekly bunch of roses
Have sufficed to keep her on track.
Too late, he would never know
On table a note topped by her band of gold
She had left her torment behind.

STOLEN LOVE

The scene was cast when our eyes met
Cross crowded room the love vibes leapt
Emotions lost in wedded mist
Came flooding back, we took the risk,
A stolen hug, a melting kiss
Tender in our secretness
With passion we much bolder grew
Weekends in motel, just for two.
It could not last it never does
Our nearest took to rave and shout.
Deception with no thought of pain
Now tears all round with us to blame,
The lives in ruins from our lust
Will end with conscience ruling us.
We took the chance as fever grew
But not for long was pleasure rich.
Now all is lost from that mad flush
Family and friends shunning us
With secret out, excitement gone
No future for that passion strong.

MIND OVER SANITY

You say it's all over
Between you and I
That your heart still belongs
But your spirit wants free
To wander and wonder
At the world and beyond
Would I be forgiving
Or my heart turn to stone.
I remember the good times
As we walked hand in hand
Also the bad times
When I cried in your arms
I wish you good luck
As you make the choice
On a heart that is steady
Or a spirit that flies.

MISSING

I need you babe to hold me
To warm my body
Through the night.
The tingle felt from your embrace
I cannot find
Though tried to chase.
A fire for you in body dwells
As into dreams
Your image steals
Remember limbs in slow motion
Speeding up
Desire in notion
Our needs from instinct
Both understood
From romantic to the crude.
Till fever hit high in the brain
To drive us on a cloud insane.
Make it back to me I pray
I need more than memory.

WHEN LOVE IS BLIND

He was told he would be sorry
The day she took his name
'but love is blind to all around
When the blood's high in the brain'
They hit the town a running
Partied dusk till dawn
Did not stop spending
Until all his cash was gone.
The honeymoon was over
She liked the glad rags on
So she up'd and did a runner
With a charmer from Coalville.
He welcomed her with open arms
When she came back to him
'For love is blind to all around
When the blood's high in the brain'
Reunion was a brief affair
She could not change her ways
D. I. V. O. R. C. E.
Was their red letter day.
Soon he wed another
As he looked for a quick fix
But it was cold between the sheets
No passion in their kiss.
He's back to being single
Searching high and low
'For love that's blind to all around
When the blood's high in the brain'

WILLOW TREE

My love is like the Willow
It bows in tune to you
When moods and passion
Shift in breeze
I sway with you to be.
To give into your deep desires
My very roots I risk
With morals, pride
Snapped as a twig
To grant your every wish.
Love is blind so they say
I know it is in me
Without this torment
In my heart
My sap with bark stands free.

THE RUN

A life for two on bobsleigh
Warm in tandem they began.
The slope was steep
With skids now on
Till death do part
Not their swan song.
Fighting, bickering, jealousy,
They fought it hard along the way
Steering straight was hard to do.
Into bends at breakneck speed
A crash was on the cards
Finally reached finishing line
Bodies battered, weary in mind.
Bobbing with the joy and strife
Such is life on bobsleigh ride.

SLICK CHICK

Always takes centre stage
Classy dresser, raver too
Built to make men's pulses race
Wriggling, giggling full of fun
Until in wedlock he ends up
SLICK CHICK.
Honeymoon now long past
Slick Chick in a spot of bother
Where's money gone from joint account?
She can't explain
Accuses him of being mean.
Now hidden spite stored up in her
Aimed at him with screaming fit
SLICK CHICK.
Starts to flirt with all and sundry
Till a toy boy she has captured.
Time for him to do a runner
Or be the doormat she is after.

THE OLD BILL

A wedge between breakers
Of man made laws
And citizens of honesty.
Die for law
On mean streets
As on wrong doers
Put the heat.
Some sights
With which they deal
Churn the stomachs
Man and female.
A minority are as bent
As those that they arrest.
To rig a statement
Not unknown.
Divorce rate high
Your wife might steal
We're only human
They then plead.
Some will cover
For a friend
Others will shop a brother.
A mixture of the human genes
Trying in honesty
To keep us clean.

SOMEONE ELSE IN BED

It should have been no surprise
The mess that he was in
Six month's courting
Three months' pregnant
Her mother hit the roof
With Daddy angry at the thought
Of his Blossom in full bloom.
They insisted on a white wedding
The wedding guests got merry
On his bank overdraft.
The first few years went quickly
Two daughters a year apart
Teaching them to walk then swim
Snowball fights in the park.
When girls reached age of puberty
He felt sort of shunned
They went all secretive
Talked only to their mum.
She got a part time city job
Made excuses to stay out late
At house warmings and such.
One morning late for work
He answered the telephone
A male voice hesitated
Then asked is Lyn at home
She streaked downstairs
Voice flustered face bright red
He knew the time had come to ask
'is someone else in bed?'

PRINCE CHARMING

He was born into a life
Of pomp and ceremony
With Butler, Footmen, Lackeys
His commands to obey
There was no doubt
He's had his fling
In many worldly ways.
She was young and pretty
With a shy downward
Bend of head
Gave a feeling of sincerity
In all she did and said.
The world watched in wonder
Their fairy tale wedding
Two sons she bore
Her charming Prince
To add to royal heirs.
In the shadows lurked
Another from the past.
When truth came out
All hell let loose
As disbelief
Through the nation rang
One question on
The world's lips
How could a fairy tale
End like this?
Divorce was on the cards.

MIND OVER PATTER

It was not in his nature
To bend knee to lady fair
Or trade in sweet platitudes
Whispered in her ear
A sense more telepathic
By gesture or look
To read in advance
The strength of her desires.
He may have been lucky
In the ladies that he met
As most prefer flattery
With a romantic flare.

STARTING AFRESH

Thanks for letting me off the hook
Of service for life to you.
A lover you had for years of two
With plans to run away with him,
No thought of what you might lose.
He let you down when truth was out
Left you in tears, life in a mess.
A whole new life in front of me
I seized the chance my mind to free
With intellectual pursuits.
Have travelled world, near and far
To view the wonderful and bizarre
Now with one of inner beauty
Learned from you cold-hearted cutie.

ALTERNATIVE LIFESTYLE

Marriage over alternative was on
Bought little house with pub and job
Three minutes' walk from home.
No more need for garden tools
Large park across the road
Where I can sit while lawns are cut
Concrete slabs round my abode,
Holidays abroad each year
My money now my own
I even eat when and what I want
And dress not as I'm told.
Cook and clean for myself
In case of a takeover.
For twenty years content I've been
Living as the wild rover,
I found myself a lady
To drive me to and from a drink
Young, virile and pretty
Pineapple juice she sips.
Now I'm getting on a bit
I might let her move in
To help me move my Zimmer Frame
When my old legs give in.
From wrestling in the bedsheets
I know I've found a dream
On my demise I hope she finds
An alternative old boy.

SKELETONS IN CUPBOARDS

The hand that gripped his shoulder
Sent shivers down the spine
Fearfully he turned to find
A stranger by his side.
Her eyes had lost all lustre
Features pale and gaunt
A sense of unease
Brought sweat upon his brow.
You know who I am she declared
I raised a child of yours
One night in lust
We took a chance
Then you disappeared.
His mind sped back four decades
When rock and roll was new
Humperdink as Dorsey
Sang in pubs he used.
Cigarettes called Woodbines
A shilling bought a pint
All the gang went Blackpool
On holiday fortnight.
Teddyboys in drainpipes
Jackets down to knees
Velvet collars, blue suede shoes
Hair brylcreemed in D.A.
Pretty chics in a twirl
Giving all a show
Of stocking tops, suspenders
As round the clock they go.
Could she be the one
Who whispered between clutch
Let's go back seat,
You don't need them

To find they could not stop.
Skeletons in cupboards
All come home to roost
Cling to weak flesh
Will give no rest
From adolescent youth.

ALONE AT CHRISTMAS

I was alone on Christmas Day
Don't shed a tear
For this is what I planned for
To escape the hue and cry
I had the usual invites
From family tree and friends
Even strangers with frayed elbows
Leaning on pub bars.
Got out of bed when I felt fit
With lunch cooked night before
Five minutes heated in microwave
It's not a day for chores.
Watched an hour of tele
Played my own CDs
Read good book, had a snooze
With just myself to please.

On Boxing day I did the rounds
Of all good friends I know
There was no doubt some had fell out
Some skint, some ill, some low.
Young Susan is not happy
With bicycle wrong colour
No five speed gear with clutch
On Yo-Yo for her brother.
A grandad ate till bloated
Then threw up in the bath
An Andrew did full Monty
His wife is raving mad.
You may think I'm selfish
But Christmas Day gave me the chance
To escape from all the hassle
That Santa Claus can cause.

FORGIVE AND FORGET

As years go by most look at past
In a different light
Old scores and scars don't matter
Optimism drives them on.
Memories relived
Could break hearts
Contentment tear apart.
To them life is the future
Looking for new horizons
As each day goes by.
Nature is a kindly foe
As they get older
Wiser and mellow grow.

HOLIDAYS SCENIC AND HUMOROUS

IN FLIGHT

No greater joy to man than this
To whisk you round the world.
Fly like a bird in an armchair
With seat belt on forget all care
Stewardess will approach
On you a pillow try to coax
You do not mind this interlude
With all her charm in action.
At intervals come
With meals and drinks
As you look forward
To holiday sun.
Toilets may have a queue
A lot of drink goes down the loo.
With Radio and Television
When flight's on time
The way to travel.

ISLAND IN THE SKY

When flying high above cloud cover
A strange new land below unfolds
You could be at the North Pole
With snow capped surface down below
Down Crevasses you can stare
Sometimes a glimpse of Mother Earth.
The sun shines down on all this
Glinting off white clouds and mist.
If on horizon eyes go search
On misty ocean pupils berth
Breathtaking, desolate virgin waste
This Island in sky has earth embraced.

ESCANA

Playa Sol Apartments overlook the sea
In a sheltered bay,
Rooms with comfort to enjoy
With little or no noise.
The staff in Restaurant
Wait to please
As you view harbour, sea and beach.
On the front small boats fill
For peaceful trips around the coast.
By Bull's Head pub
A scenic walk is in sight
Wild flowers by a pathway
Lead to another Bay
Which is just visible
Through the trees.
Nightly pleasure you can find
With Barbecue of beaten track
Karaoke, Disco or pubs with Quiz
All are there to take your pick.
If feeling a bit romantic
Panorama Hotel will set the mood.

SQUELCH

At sixteen left family home
To seek the sun abroad did roam.
Any squat was his front door
Till speak strange tongue
Could get no more.
To keep himself smelling fresh
Clothes and all in swim pools tread
When in tatter from all this,
Hippie market clothes to fix.
Rides a moped with donkey bag
Seeking any work can have.
To apartment did ascent
On cleanliness in shower hellbent,
Squelching, thumping with his feet
From sweaty clothes
The dust to beat.
With Mick and Tich from city Leicester
Drinks the wine, plays the jester,
Of the beauties had his share
But moves before they get in hair.
If into squelch in Ibiza bump,
Young maids into hot water jump.

THE COCKNEYS

She met them on holiday
With their wives had come to stay
Mates for life they had been
No cross words passed between,
With wives, pleasant and good fun.
Work for men was milky way
Told old tales of horse and dray.
In Ibiza town they bought a book
Much in decay,
From its depths they could recall
Tales with which all would enthral
Barman Minola often outwit
With Spanish folklore
From the book.
With them she drank through a straw
A mixture named Burner still on flame.
Short arms long pockets
Was not their way
They paid all night with Cockney sway.

EDDIE AND ROSIE

He is a boxer like his dad
Champion of junior fame.
Three hundred fights at different weights
For opponents was checkmate.
Stage struck at the time was Rosie
But with Eddie did not pose.
Off abroad they did go
To run a pub with some show.
Entertained with songs and tricks
With tourists were a hit.
Rosie's cooking is well known
For keeping body in good tone.
Villains like all have met a few
But get respect they are due.
Now own bar with pool to swim
To lift the spirits
Cool the limbs.

CAROL BILLIE

Sitting with a drink in the sun
On a holiday relaxing
Last thing on her mind
A toy boy or romance.
Two youths with attitude
Sat down at her table.
Bold and sure of themselves
No thought of rejection dwelt.
Her answer to one's request to bed
Left him all a fluster.
'You young studs are really dumb
My body is not for your fun
I am old enough to be your mum
I need respect and maturity
Not two yobs after a takeaway.'

NO WAY

Neat petite from head to feet
With big blue eyes
Your heart to eat,
Would adorn any stately room
Powerful and rich would surely swoon.
A child like beauty of eighteen
In Spanish bar sits so serene,
Her eyes are riveted
Deep longing there
On handsome youth
With long dark hair.
He chats the ladies, serves them drinks
But from her gaze
His eyes shrink.
For it's the men he loves to meet
She's just a floozie in a seat.
In years to come will surely blush
When thinks for gay
Her blood did rush.

SHERLENE

New Zealand reared to maturity
Tours the world with spirit free
Works her way to each country
To see first hand with clarity.
In London, Israel, Cyprus, Cairo
Experiences the mind to grow
Has many scares as well as thrills
This daring young lady
With smile inbuilt.
Lover lives on a Kabbutz
Not yet her wish
To set down roots.

RYTHMY

Nationalities of all kinds
Broke the silence, with the wine
In this bar in Limassol
Philosopher, beauty, poet too
Of the world gave points of view.
Flags of nations were discussed
Without any angry outbursts
It was a change to say the least
Not to be threatened by beliefs.

RASTA AND ESTA
SPIT ROAST

Me an ma waman Esta an a vacashan gat inta a situashan. An first day in da sun gat a hunga far grub an fun. Buys a chikan af a da spit, Wak alang with fingas eatan it. Juicas drip dan ma chin onta gold chain an a dan ma front, Estas sun tap getan a stained. Slip inta a Disco bar, lickan fingas, smackan da lips an a spitan da roast. Gatan inta da haladay mood, flashan with da camara. Swigan, gulpan dan da drinks big feet a thampan ta da beat. Esta an da Rum an black starts ta flash har bady parts, than strips dan ta bra an pants. D.J.man give as angra tak as ansa ham by cussan back. Bouncer man as eyeballs than ham tak a swing at me. Esta double ham with knee, shuv ham face inta da chikan left an tray. Grab Esta's nick nacks an sun tap, dash with da camara far da exat. Ran dan tha street, dance an, shoutan like two o dem crazy lagar mans. Ma blood na boilan fram al tha excitemant, but Esta gat har glad rags back an. Jump inta da hotel swiman pool, in wet san tap, Esta look real cool. A taks ma waman by da hand, ta relax man an siesta in apartmant.

JACK THE LAD

What can a say lads
I've been and done it all
On the Costa Brava
And the Costa Del Sol
I've also been to Rhodes
And the Isle of Kos
Cyprus, Israel and Egypt
Farther afield can also boast.
Everywhere I've sang and danced
With the English rose
Even felt I might have caught
More than just a cold.
Now find the rose a put off
As she staggers from Disco
And with a flip of mini skirt
Bare bum to me she shows.
I'd rather see a class act
Like the one that we all know
Benidorm 'Sticky Vicky'
A legend coast to coast.
She must be a Great Granny now
But she still can see her toes
As she discreetly conjures out
Razor Blades, Flags and Cards
From partly hidden crevice
At early morning shows.

HOLIDAY MED
DELAYED FLIGHT HOME

At the end of holiday
By twelve noon room to vacate.
As flight home is at midnight
All day to wait and hang about.
Airport filled to the doors
Delays showing on the board
People drunk and up are throwing
Kids are screaming, tired and bored
To ears bedlam, eyes a fright.
Food and drink priced sky high
Afraid to queue in crush might die
Nowhere can you sit your bum
On floors lie bodies by the score.
French Air Controllers are on strike
To coincide with British holidays
It happens most summer breaks
A price for sun you have to take.

VICTIMIZATION OF THE INNOCENT

After decades of soft authority, with discipline abandoned, the breakdown of British society and culture, shows no sign of slowing down. Human rights appears to be in favour of those with criminal intent, while victims of injustice are treated with contempt. The state has tied the hands of those who should control, the cotton wool wrapped generation who crass and brass now act. Honest, stealth taxed citizens who for this country fought and slaved, are at the back of queue, for everything, this welfare state was made.

DISCIPLINE (BRITISH STYLE)

Ten year olds murdered
A little lad of two
Educated and pampered
Now in secret live as free.
Other kids running wild
Smoke, drink, sniff pots of glue.
Extortion by the bully
Now out of control
Of innocent heads, suicide roll call.
Elders live in fear and stress
Of the child they once held dear.
Threaten to smack a child of yours
Of social services beware.
The days have long gone
When punishment fitted the crime
And law and order was respected.

THE WAY IT IS

The sun filtered through
The vertical blinds
On to the dusty sill
Before stretching across
The muck stained veneer
Of the dining table,
Cobwebs decorated with trappings
Hung like curtains
From corners of the room.
The body sat
In solitary confinement
Glimpses of the ribs
Stood out in sharp contrast
To the rotting flesh.
Days of neighbourly compassion
Were now a distant memory.
A crowbar lay by the front door
Thankfully the staring eyes
Were now blind to reality
And the floor now strewn
With a lifetime of treasured memories
But worthless items
To the heartless vultures of today.

INNER CITY THUG
(BRITISH)

Walks into pub swings baseball bat
Lands a hit on landlord's head,
Smashes furnishings with great speed.
Already he has had fun day
Glassed his dad and knocked him out,
After threatening all inside
With drugged up eyes he walks away.
Panic button pressed to summon help,
From police station.
Sixty minutes later
Two officers arrive.
'You say he is a Mason named Kerry
Does he have a brother called Perry?
Landlord not amused by this
Asks if they have been on speed,
'Landlord if you charge this man
Form filling for us will be bad
Please write it off as accident,
Revenge by druggie
Not what you want'

PRODIGAL

Alone in bed
The creak on stairs
She heard with dread.
He stood in doorway
A masked face in the gloom
Threatened with a knife
She handed over handbag and purse.
As he bent to inspect
Ill gotten gains
The mask slipped off his evil face,
The man was her only son.
Fifteen months to prison sent
He could not suppress a grin.
If sanity in courts prevailed
He would forever rot in jail.

TECHNIQUE

Leave your car for half an hour
To have a drink or take a shower,
Car unlocked stereo gone.
Now locks been upgraded
A new way been found,
Rod through letter box
Takes car keys outside.
But now the thief
Has upped the crime
With a buyer for your car.
It won't be long before they find
Ways to move your house
With you inside.
Modern technology in full sting.

BABY JOE

You know him as well as I
On every street he walks by,
Breaks into houses at age ten
Causing terror and mayhem.
Now six foot four a born thug
With knife or gun maims and mugs
Holds up young mothers pushing prams
Give me your money or baby hangs.
Throws petrol bombs when in tantrums
Then runs home to loving mum
Law then provides him with holiday
Do gooders with our taxes pay.

THE YOB AND STEAL SOCIETY

Roll the joint, smoke the dope
Wrap my brains in overcoat
Drink the booze, lose control
Temper hits danger zone
Go on ecstasy, in a daze
Slavery from my own free will.
Take joy ride in someone's car
No tax, insurance, what a laugh
Three best mates died in crash.
Six of us on to one
Put the boot in, play the thug
Grannies cower when they see us.
On a gang bang, hold bird down
She asked for it, out late at night
Scratch cars, set fire to schools
Break into property, then we trash
Steal anything on order sheet
Buyer waits with wad in fist.
We've taken over, we now rule
Parents now under our control.
If not show us enough respect
Bullet or Shaftin, you will get.

THE ENVIRONMENT

As we are continually reminded by our elite, the environment is in a mess. With egoistic, sleaze-ridden Politicians, Dictators and Despots, lavishly fed, pampered, protected and on an endless gravy train, the future for us all looks bleak. The authoritarian rule of Communism, The Taliban and religious zealots of all creeds is also not the answer. There must be found a newer, greener, middle ground that is fairer to all. Or are we to be reeled into oblivion by words that have been twisted through the years, out of all recognition, from books written in the dark ages, and the John Lewis list mentality of our elite.

GREENPEACE

When environment disaster
Hits earth or sea
These dedicated few
Turn up to toil.
There activities sometimes
Cause a great outcry
From Governments
That they upset.
An inspiring battle
They also fight
For creatures other
Than Mankind.

HERITAGE

From roots entrenched
In healthy soil
Thrusts stem for vine,
To flourish forth,
The fruit and scent
Of living bloom,
By sun enriched
Through warmth of noon,
With rain to feed
The roots below
Mankind's fulfilment
If nurtured so.

SUMMER

It's come again
Though took long time
Now feeds the fruits
Of root and vine.
White waxed skin
To pink will go
If sun too much
Red face can glow.
Use the sun cream
One and all
For cancer screen
From ozone hole.

ACID

It can be good or harmful
For us all it has some pull
A substance which is in much use
In little pill can turn brain loose.
If around the body lapped
Will eat the flesh from front to back.
As a mino acid it is known
To help the hair, head to adorn.
In vinegar it gives the food
A flavour mouth likes to include.
Acid drops are bottle sweets
To refresh taste buds hard to beat.
As man-made rain it rots the trees
Nature finds it hard to please.
We mortals hits
With stomach pain
Or to the chest
With burn it canes
If married to an acid tongue
A life of torment has begun.

SAND

It comes in many a different hue
With uses that are far from few
As on a beach you soak up sun
A golden stretch to lay at leisure.
Children mix it with sea water
Into a castle it can alter.
Three to one mix with cement
Changes into a concrete.
All sort of glass from sand made
Some with names to be engraved.
Poured into canvas bags
Helps keep flood water at bay.
With it in sandpit kids can play
When far away from the seashore.
Gives smooth texture to the wood
As sandpaper rubbed on crude.
Around the world large quantities lie
How long will this be so?
With man about
Might shrink or grow.

THE SEEKERS

In bowels of earth
Dark tremors of the deep
Mankind in search
Not yet complete.
To suck into his treasure chest
All nature bestows
In trust to let.
Voracious the appetite of man
As into throat
The spoils he rams.

SURVIVAL

America land of the dream
Haven for so many gene,
With world in turmoil to the core
Salvation stems from White House door.
Dark shadows in power mad heads
Tears and blood of innocent shed.
In withered skins with jutting bones
From drought and genocide millions roam.
Religious dogma stalks the soul
With bomb or bullet terrorists call.
Pollution saps Mother Nature's strength
As day by day she chokes on stench.
We lay a shroud over tree and bloom
Through ozone hole watch sun or moon.
Are we so primitive destructively insane
That from our source life blood we drain.
To save all species from extinct,
In united state turn back from brink.

THE BRINK

Ignorance, Intolerance
Lies deep in human race
As with a will it sets about
Destruction of the land.
By billions spawn the human throng
To scrape earth bare, night and dawn
While granny Smith contracts with glee
From science induced fertility.
As earth decays a ray of hope
With water found on Mars.
The Universe in terror waits
Watches with great awe
Man's giant leap into space
Other Worlds to destroy.

WORKING TOGETHER

Toiling in harmony all as one
For fuller life to be won.
Offering to others a helping hand
Instead of hoarding what we can.
A little time to sacrifice
For those down trodden in our eyes,
Richer in spirit we can be
By showing some charity.
Like most of us I've done some wrong
As no saint was I born,
But I like you can start afresh
By giving more while taking less.

RELIGION

ADAM AND EVE

From the dust came Adam
For the modelling of Eve
Constructed for harmony
But flawed to deceive.
From incestuous start
By the word we are told
The human family
To this world evolved.
If this is so we are as one
Why were we cloned
To kill and stun.
Greed and envy, hate to lust
Emotions from depth of hell in us
Love with pity, caring we do
A heaven and hell
On earth in view.

THE TEN COMMANDMENTS

In judgement book
We are told
Is record of
All sin and shame.
If repentance of these
On earth declared
You walk with ease
Through pearly gates
If not your soul
For eternity
In burning fire
Of Hell will stay.

THE ONE AND ONLY

In great anger
Immortal looks upon
His creation
Named Mankind.
He blessed them
With a fertile brain
They tuned it high
To kill and maim,
He wrote a book
With wisdom full
They twisted script
As broke each rule.
The end is near
Say prophets of doom
He will not forever
Just watch and fume.

MORTALS

Burdened down with earthly sins
Who put them there not clear.
We rape, pillage, annihilate
Religion's name put to shame,
Concern about a life,
Hereafter
Makes our existence
A disaster.

THE PREACHERS

They come in different disguises
To enlighten, frighten and chastise
Read out Gospel from religious book.
Some speak of Brimstone and Damnation
Others of Virgins in waiting.
Wise words written for our good
Used on weak willed by the scheming.
A few in expensive business suits
With flashy wives, mansions build
Bought with money from converts
A couple in prison now domiciled.
For sexual perversions others go down
With blind eyes turned by their peers.
Some against equality of the sexes
Think only men can reach our senses.
Others with power gone to head
Think are Immortal one on earth.
A lot of good some of them do
But safer to read and think for self.

THE SALVATION ARMY

The mightiest force known to man
Recruits of all nations in their ranks
Its battle banners stretch worldwide
Without a blood stain on the mind.
The rank and file work night or day
Collecting for all charity.
Officers on paltry pay
Lead from front on missions grey
No bomb or bullet do they use
But with a news sheet air their views
If ever you are down and out
Soup, tea with bun, warm comfort shout
No preaching they of right or wrong
Or with the bible come on strong.
A bed in hostel will provide
With eggs and bacon sunny side.
When dying on life's battlefield
Always on hand to hold and shield
Your soul is safe within their ranks
All the world owe them thanks.

DUMB DUMBS

Snipers sights aimed in cold blood
With Dum, Dum bullets ready
Christian, Atheist, Muslim, Jew,
Hindu, Agnostic, Buddha Priest
No matter what beliefs you teach
Dum, Dum bullets are for you.
Target at random adult or child
Killing streets of blood in style.
As we all are ethnic to some degree
Dumb Dumb extinction for all is key
The Devil dances a merry jig
As his disciples terror preach
In any manner they see fit.

POLITICS

ALIENS

Creatures made from puff and blow
Wrapped in thick skins to protect ego
Working tool a glib tongue
From which the nation's fate is hung
Pure and white they may appear
But to the whip all do adhere
Toe sucking minority with innocent air
Never a blush in public glare.
Promises they make galore
Then with a u-turn close the door
A taxing time with little joy
Aliens blowing off top soil.

QUESTION TIME

Order! Order!
The speaker shouts
At the unruly mob
As they sit down, stand up
Drown each other out,
A toe curling spectacle
In public view.
These are responsible adults
At the country's helm
Why do they need headmaster
Each bench to quell?
Labour back benchers
In fawning submission
Quote party achievements
As their questions.
When leader cornered
By opposition bench
Recalls obscure facts
When they were not in power.
Tony Blair was master at this
A cheap con trick to diverse.
In their fairy tale world
We all know
They cannot answer
Yes! or No!

BLOOD OF BLUES

What bad example they can be
To those with ears and eyes to see.
For centuries have lived our lords
Watching over starving hordes.
Give aura to all of purity
While in their rightful beds.
Affairs with ladies or male friends
To their debauchery is no end.
On freebies live fringe family
Digging into workers' pay,
Brainwashed into needing them
When from our sweat their riches spent.
If found out and guilt is ripe
Come on hard with charity might
Preach to us what we should do
To help the skinny out of stew.
We know you will not
Change your ways
Population fed up
With sex and sleaze.

MONEY

We treat it in so many ways
To some it's there to spend as please
Others with scrooge mentality
In sweaty palm hold it tightly.
You work hard to coin nest egg
To find it makes a life of stress.
By phone, internet, junk mail,
Lotteries and credit cards
Even stock market registration
On British nation World's conmen call.
They know we all are fair game
With government and law out of touch
And not enough jails to lock them up.
Easier and safer to spend nest egg
And live off social benefits.

TAXMAN

He calls on you at anytime
To turn your life upside down.
Tries to screw you to the floor
Where did each coin have it's core.
Usually hits when times are low
With bills piling up to go.
If business out of tune
Tries to make you bankrupt soon.
Send forms none to clear
Which causes grey and loss of hair.
Searches into every nitch
Were you left money by Cousin Fitz.
Leech like clings to you,
In case some wealth you do stow.
Wants to know from your lips
If your bank has tight grip.
All the time he's after you
His bosses prime you to make do.

HOUSE TAX REBATE

As a single occupier
Council tax reduction overlooked,
Until this letter
He sent to the council
Through the mail.
'I am a man of forty five
Who lives alone as if in heaven.
I have no lady, live within
Last one nailed me to the floor.
I do not keep a dog or cat
Or have as paying guest a pal.
You check out my every move
From eye in sky, street cameras,
Telephone and knock on door.
Are you into magic now
To make my rebate disappear?'

THE JOB

Two years' wait, rain gets in
Water drips in buckets and tins
Replacement window at last arrives
Day off work to supervise.
To plaster round window no can do
Council will send another crew.
Another day lost, note hits floor,
Estimate needed to do this chore
Week later estimate made
Finish of job still delay
Do these people really get paid?
When finally you can decorate
Maybe that will lift the gloom.
If all red tape had knots undone
A princely saving would be won.

RETIREMENT

A lifetime of slavery
To a clock
At last you're free.
No more rushing to and fro
As the seconds quickly flow.
A late breakfast
Or time on the loo
Without the dread of being late.
You worked hard to save
Holidays you now can take
At any time or place.
'Timeout' to swim and chat
To do whatever the hell you please,
Shopping trips not now a pain
Thanks to tick tock
Off wrist and shelf.

MEMORIES

Can't live on them
But you can reflect
On things of joy or living hell.
One moment it's all deep gloom
Pockets empty, clothes in shreds
Lose lover, family or a friend.
Then you hit a lucky streak
Soon felt like a millionaire.
You reached forty, crises in mind
But why on earth should you feel blue,
To the Graham and Josephine
Remember as your lives unfold
Enjoy it all before it goes.
Millions less fortunate than you
Would be more than pleased
To fill your shoes.

QUALITY OF LIFE

Blessed am I to be alive
Healthy in mind and body
Imagination on increase
Memories not started to recede.
With fading eyes I still view
The world in awe and wonder
My sense of smell still inhales
All of nature's bounty
Hearing is not impaired
To slightest sound alerted.
Teeth and taste buds
Stood test of time
I eat what's recommended
Exercise keeps limbs supple
Blessed then am I
With extra muscle.
The will to live life
To the full
Triumphs over every trial.

THE SOCK COMPANY

We wish you in retirement
A rest from stress and toil
A life filled with pleasure
Enjoyed to the full.
You could be a little pompous
But never were you rude
A gentleman in manner
With morals of the good.
Your job in charge of quality
Of socks made by the best
When socks got tight
Or rather slack
You gave the best no rest.
We will all miss you
For waiting in the wings
We know there is another
With much more potent sting.

ROSEDENE, PECKLETON

She sat in sheltered garden
As the leaves around her fell
Lawn covered in gold and brown
As mother nature turned cold.
From Walnut tree the nuts lay
Squirrels scurried to and fro.
En masse the birds swarmed
Heading for a warmer clime.
A Hedgehog walks to summer house
Its refuge when cold winter calls.
House bricks a mass of colour
From red and yellow ivy cover
Conifer trees sway in the breeze
Looking down on potting shed.
Brussel Boy statue by garden loo
Now flowers have wilted in full view.
From ornamental wall on terrace
The Gnome family survey it all.
As with dusk the scene grows dim
She walks up path of Cornish Slate
Content to cook the evening meal
The memory will live on within.

WASTE-AGE

As she looked back on her life
She shed a tear
For wasting her capacity
In brain and body.
She could have done so many things
With an intellect equal to most.
But safely in the life of a plodder
In business, romance and adventure
Curbed her desires.
She thought wistfully,
No one with the gift of life
Should be here to just exist.

THE RIM

As tyre starts to thin
Only way headed is the rim
For human race alike
In circle life does go
Strong start to falter
As inner tube does blow,
Make most of tread
While in good trim
Satisfaction from life
You then will win.

THREE IN ONE

At eighteen the world
Is her plaything
Whatever disguise
She may come in
Can manipulate the male hormone
Blush or brash can cause a storm,
At forty if kept in trim
She still reigns supreme
Security with love now mixed
In comfort zone
She finds her kicks.
At seventy has earned respect
For years of care of family set
No longer attracts with sex appeal
But can disarm with a smile.
There are exceptions to the rule
But why should I be kind or cruel.

RESIDENTIAL AND NURSING HOME

Sally and John
Run their two part home
With great efficiency.
Sally has a ready smile
Comforting in manner.
Husband John has gentle tone
As residents he visits.
The staff are dedicated
In following their lead
A credit to their career path
Discreet in their tasks
Patient and understanding.
As relative of a past resident
I write these words
With thanks.

VISITING TIME

Grey heads nod in unison
The whiff of stale urine
Hard to suppress.
Millie greets you hands outstretched
Rising unsteadily on ulcered legs
'Nurse me master, nurse me,' Her plea for a hand to hold.
Elizabeth shuffles by, unaware
Of a rapid burping from her rear.
Derick as always never still
Still living as a business king
'Move your legs stupid cow'
His imagined trip four days behind.
Long legged Ann wrapped in shawl
Mi heads cold, oh dear mi heads cold
Dum de dum de dum dum drones in song.
Marie's frail frame does a feeble jig
Got to get me fat off
I a naughty girl insists.
On Mick's trousers spreads a stain
Oblivious to young carer's charm
As helped off to comfort change.
Visiting awakes you to the fact
The hands of time no one can grasp.

ON THE SUBJECT OF DEATH
AND LIFE AFTER

THE BELIEVERS

People who appear to need the comforting belief that their existence goes on after death. Many are taught from the cradle that their parents' religion, or its breakaway arm, is the only way to immortality. Others are convinced of contact from beyond the grave, the sudden unexpected aroma of a departed relations favourite tobacco, or perfume. Light switches which had been put to the off position the night before, for some strange reason in the switched on position in the morning. Even ghosts in well known, worn suits, shoes, or dresses, bought by loved ones. To speak to the photo or even the ashes of a very close one, can also renew someone's faith in a future reunion. No positive proof has yet stepped from beyond the grave to give us a true insight to our fate. On this subject I sit on the fence in deep contemplation. If there is a life after death, the two well narrated extremes, which gave me nightmares as a five year old, do not appeal to my comfort zone. A more natural paradise for myself would be a centre path, with a little suffering along the way. This to help me appreciate the good from the bad, leading to a lush green plateau, where I could rest my slightly sinful head, in the comfort of a soft ample bosom. Come to think about it, I may already be as close to Heaven as one can get.

No matter what the circumstance, regardless of age or sex, for those left behind, death is stressful and a reminder of our own lifeless fate. For this reason I thought it right that examples of the Grim Reaper should contain a little humour through Father Bobby and Humpty Dumpty.

PRINCESS AND QUEEN

So much to give
Taken so soon
A flower plucked
From us
In full bloom.
Disabled, sick and dying
She comforted with a smile
Compassion was her forte
With elegance and style.
We laid a wreath
With tears of grief
It stretched the World wide
For she was special
One apart
Princess Diana Queen of Hearts.

JADE

She was a product
Of our time
From back streets
To media star
With no trace of talent
To go far.
Fame and good fortune
Followed quick,
Then got involved
In a confrontation
That brought trouble
Between two nations.
Misfortune then multiplied
With Cervical cancer terminal
In the weeks before
Jade's demise
In pain she put on
A brave face,
Her thoughts for those
She would leave behind
Made many see her
In a different light.
The good in her
Was there to see
A shame it showed
With tragedy.

MADNESS

Brakes scream, engines fume
Impatient to the point of doom.
Hard down on pedal, accelerate
Oblivion for some who wary wait.
On motorway all hell let loose
Truck, bus and car
Have breakneck blues,
Metal grinds metal, sparks ignite
Trapped human flesh set alight
Screams of terror, horror reigns
From folly of uncaring brain.

JENNIE

By chance he met her in Dunfermline Glen
On a visit to his place of birth.
The childhood girl he had adored
Was blessed with beauty in womanhood
They lost no time in making up
For years apart that they had lost.
One day they walked to Fife's Loch Leven
A place of solitude a haven
On an Island there with pulses throbbing
They planned their future as they lay.
Next day would be Jennie's last
A victim in a multiple car crash.
They buried her in Ballingry cemetery
On a warm summer's day
As years go by she stays in mind
For in his head has built a shrine
To a life cut short by fate unkind.

KATH

We wish you well
In this time of stress
To us you are
As a friend the best.
Don't let the treatment
Get you down
We're always near
In spirit sound.
With sense of humour
That you have
You will we know
Turn smile from sad.
Like a sister to me
As we chat things through
From Sherl and Mick
Good health to you.

DEPARTED

The mind has lost control
Since from my life you softly stole.
I miss soft tresses, eyes of blue
But most of all sharp wit in you.
Memories of times we had
In notes and letters bring you back.
Life will never be the same
My loss of you is heaven's gain.

TILL DEATH DO PART

From childhood friend
To teenage lover, to wife with grace
You bore our fruit,
Taught good from bad
Had patience when
From straight I strayed.
With wisdom kept the family close.
From bud to blossom in full bloom
Then taken from us
Much to soon.

SWITCHED OFF

You left me so suddenly
From full of life
To dead same day.
No time to whisper fond goodbye
For happiness that you gave
We met so young, wed real quick
So many years a life so rich.
No tears shed as time flew by
Only contentment in each sigh.
We kept so pure the vows we made
With no other did betray.
Will meet again of that I'm sure
Belief so strong
Pain can endure.

THE HARROD'S BAG

To Dave Smith a symbol of prestige
His few belongings in which to squeeze
He sailed the seas all alone
With Harrod's bag he felt at home.
Boat wrecked in ninety two
With Portinax within view,
People grew to love the man
Who from the ocean had strongly swam,
In bars Features and Mirramar
Drank till tongue lost all grammar.
Friends tried to talk him off the drink
But he always had a thirst to quench.
To sail to Australia was his dream
Into the wind the sail to lean
Dave found face down in the sea
Harrod's bag floating in the bay.

SHIPWRECKED

The waves surge onto the shore
Gaunt jutting rocks engulf.
As wind tears through the rigging
In shreds the sails are hung.
Rain and spray blurs vision
Of now exhausted crew,
With helm out of control
Disaster only view.
The rocks bite into timbered bow
With groan the mast gives way,
Those trapped beneath
The sea will swamp
Into its depths this day.

DEATH IN BOSNIA

They died on steps defending home
Their bodies then burnt
Through to the bone
Four children with a terrified mum
Huddled together in smoke filled room
Smelt the deaths, they soon would share.
Religion again its good name stained
As an excuse for ethnic cleansing,
Another holocaust in the making
Have we returned to the dark ages.
This insanity round world carries on
As power mad Despots feast on greed.

LET LOOSE

From killing on all parts of globe
Red haze rises
The stench mind blows
As human predator takes its toll
Attacks from deep in heart and soul.
Manipulation of our genes
May one day cleanse
Illness and terror
From our dreams.

FATHER-BOBBY

Bones splintered in arm and hand
After years of knocks and hits
From at coal face with pick.
Trapped under pit roof collapse
For day and night was feared dead
Dragged out with a broken leg.
As widower when retired
Up at dawn to clean and cook.
Played dominoes with friends
Tilly and Harold
With his wits drove them silly.
Wrote a book aged eighty two
Of family tree and life he knew.
Was a live wire on party nights
When he downed glasses of stout.
In high collared white tee shirt
One day mistaken for a priest
Why did the lady blush
As she left him?
He would not tell, as he grinned
Their conversation safe with him.
His humour and goodwill
Remembered by all he knew.

THE SILENT SHADOW

Created by shades of light
Attired in sombre black
Each object still or moving holds
In light but blends with dark.
The shades of light its master
Will stretch front, or behind you
Or shrink in its disguise.
In lonely house
Confronts you on the wall
Can still your breath
This silent shape
Make heart beat fast from slow.
Never of much comfort
As it flits, distorts round you
To merge or disappear
When shades of light are few.
You can reach out to touch it
But it has no substance
In feel or human smell
It follows in your movement
In twin with hand that twitches
Or head that bends to shoe
What is this silent shadow?
A devil from the darkest pit
Or soul in heaven's trust
Its secret lies in hazy heat
The greyness of the dawn
Will it depart for ever
When from this life we are gone?

HUMPTY DUMPTY
EXTERMINATED

My mother looked down on me
With a worried frown
A little hump of pearly white
Most people preferred brown.
A hand slipped underneath her
Grabbed me warm as I lay
It was the beginning of the end
For me that fateful day.
They put me on a moving belt
With hundreds of my kind
Graded me as one from five
Deep yellow streak inside.
Into a box they packed me
Cracked running wounds all round
When people saw the state of us
They dumped us on one side.
Eventually bought on the cheap
To be boiled in a pan
Till I was not quite runny
Five minutes on watch hand.
I then took a bashing
From a silver spoon
Before a knife sliced off my head
To feed a human goon.
If I'd been broken, split in two
Then dropped into a fry
When turned over sunnyside
I think I would have died.

JANUARY

Looking down on the dim lit street
The emptiness and silence
Made my isolation complete.
Two cards from Christmas past
From usual greetings were missing.
Aunt Fanny departed peacefully
A smile upon her face.
Friend Chad in his prime
Crashed out in sorry state.
After a hearty breakfast
My spirits began to soar
As I contemplated my blessings
Instead of life no more.
I earn enough to pay my way
My needs are not excessive.
Envy is not in my mind
Or material goods to cherish.
Imagination fills the void
Of all that's gone before.
Poetry led it must be said
A new world to discover
In historical prints, children's books
Short stories and a novel.

Blessed am I with words to try
To justify my being.

ADDRESSING THE VERSE

At a poets' convention
In Washington D.C.
A Senator Macarthy
Addressed the jamboree.
'Once a poet, always a poet
A captive you are held
It brings more meaning
To your life than
Riches, power or health'
Rod Steiger of film fame
A millionaire in truth
Was asked what now
His aim in life
In hour long interview.
I would give up all
Without a doubt
In life that I've achieved
To write one famous verse,
That I would be remembered by
When I depart this earth
Dylan Thomas, Burns and Keats
All have attained Rod's goal
Sadly it only happens
To a gifted few we know.
Pam Eyres with her humour
Will also leave her mark
She proved to all and sundry
That poets also laugh.
Poetry gives the freedom

Imagination to unwind
To take you down paths unknown
On subjects of all kinds,
Brings out by words, in a way
No pill or potion can
The stress that builds
In mind and gut
As fate deals you its hand.
It gives you peace
An inner joy
A cleansing of your soul
Dark secrets held
In depths of brain
Fast to the surface flow.
We are kindred spirits
From all walks of life
As we address the verse
A benefit to mankind.

THE NEARLY MAN –
IN QUESTION

Would born with a silver spoon
Have broadened my horizons
Or ambition fed brought on stress
To start a chain reaction?
Might I have been a statesman
Believing in my spin
Or courting sleaze and vice
To bridge the gap between?
If I had reached the pinnacle
As a novel writer
Would I have slipped, lost my grip
As critics pulled me under?
Creativity by connection
Put in the spotlight
Millionaire or weakest link
No doubt would find me out.
As a sporting personality
My nature leans to Jack the Lad
Not training with desire.
If the ladies in my life
Belonged to upper crust
Would they be put off?
A nearly man in limbo
Paranoid of great divide.

PUZZLED

What guides the pen
To write a phrase
From beginnings deep
In subconscious maze.
To gather words
While half awake
Then nurture them
Till sense they make.
I only know
That it is so
As mind on pillow
Wakes to flow?

Lightning Source UK Ltd.
Milton Keynes UK
30 March 2010

152120UK00001B/7/P